K-PAX

K·PAX

gene brewer

BLOOMSBURY

First published in Great Britain in 1995

Bloomsbury Publishing plc, 38 Soho Square, London, W1D 3HB

A CIP catalogue record for this book is available from the British Library

ISBN 0 7475 5752 7

10 9 8 7 6 5 4

Printed in Great Britain by Clays Ltd, St Ives plc

When we successfully treat a patient . . . we experience a burst of joy because we have helped a suffering person who is happy to have known us. But we also feel a secret joy, because we have come to know him, and in knowing him we know more of ourselves.

—SYLVANO ARIETI

Prologue

I N April, 1990, I received a call from Dr. William Siegel at the Long Island Psychiatric Hospital. Bill is an old friend of mine, and a distinguished colleague. On this particular occasion the call was a professional one.

Bill was treating a patient who had been at the hospital for several months. The patient, a white male in his early thirties, had been picked up by the New York City police after being found bending over a mugging victim in the Port Authority Bus Terminal in midtown Manhattan. According to their report his answers to routine questions were "daffy" and, after they booked him, he was taken to Bellevue Hospital for evaluation.

Although he was somewhat emaciated, medical examination revealed no organic abnormality, nor was there evidence of formal thought disorder, aphasia, or auditory hallucination, and he presented a near-normal affect. However, he did harbor a rather bizarre delusion: He believed he came from another planet. After a few days' observation he was transferred to Long Island, where he remained for the next four months.

Bill was unable to do much for him. Although he remained alert and cooperative throughout the various courses of treatment, the patient was completely unresponsive to the most powerful antipsychotic drugs. At the end of it all he remained firmly convinced that he was a visitor from "K-PAX." What was worse, he was able to enlist many of his fellow patients to this fantasy. Even some of the staff were beginning to listen to him! Knowing that the phenomenology of delusion has long been an interest of mine, Bill asked me to take a crack at him.

It couldn't have come at a worse time. As acting director of the Manhattan Psychiatric Institute I was already swamped with more work than I could handle and, indeed, had been phasing out patient interaction since January of that year. However, the case sounded both interesting and unusual, and I owed Bill a couple of favors. I asked him to send me a copy of the man's file.

When it arrived I was still bogged down by administrative duties, and a few more days went by before I found it lying on my desk under a pile of personnel and budget folders. With renewed dismay over the prospect of another patient I quickly read through the chart. It summarized a puzzling history indeed. Although our "spaceman" was quite lucid and articulate, and demonstrated a strong awareness of time and place, he was unable to provide any reliable information as to his actual origin and background. In short, he was not only delusional, but a total amnesiac as well! I called Bill and asked him to make arrangements for the transfer of this nameless man, who called himself "prot"—not capitalized—to my own institution.

He arrived the first week in May, and a preliminary session with him was scheduled for the ninth, a Wednesday, at the time I usually set aside to prepare for my regular "Principles of Psychiatry" lecture at Columbia University. We met at weekly intervals for several months thereafter. During that period I developed an extraordinary fondness and regard for this patient, as the following narrative, I trust, will show.

Although the results of these sessions have been reported in the scientific literature, I am writing this personal account not only because I think it might be of interest to the general public but also, to paraphrase Dr. Arieti, because of what he taught me about myself.

Session One

My first impression, when he was brought into my examining room, was that he was an athlete—a football player or wrestler. He was a little below average in height, stocky, dark, perhaps even swarthy. His hair was thick and coal-black. He was wearing sky-blue corduroy pants, a denim shirt, and canvas shoes. I didn't see his eyes for the first few encounters; despite the relatively soft lighting, he always wore dark glasses.

I asked him to be seated. Without a word he proceeded to the black vinyl chair and sat down. His demeanor was calm and his step agile and well coordinated. He seemed relaxed. I dismissed the orderlies.

I opened his folder and jotted the date on a clean yellow pad. He watched me quite intently, evincing a hint of a smile. I asked him whether he was comfortable or needed anything. To my surprise he requested an apple. His voice was soft but clear, with no detectable regional or foreign accent. I buzzed our head nurse, Betty McAllister, and asked her to see if there were any available in the hospital kitchens.

While we waited I reviewed his medical record: Temperature, pulse, blood pressure, EKG, and blood values were all within the normal range, according to our chief clinic physician, Dr. Chakraborty. No dental problems. Neurological exam (muscle strength, coordination, reflexes, tone) normal. Left/right discrimination normal. No problem with visual acuity, hearing, sensing hot or cold or a light touch, handling platonic solids, describing pictures, copying figures. No difficulty in solving complex problems and puzzles. The patient was quick-witted, observant, and logical. Except for his peculiar delusion and total amnesia, he was as healthy as a horse.

Betty came in with two large apples. She glanced at me for approval and, when I nodded, offered them to the patient. He took them from the little tray. "Red Delicious!" he exclaimed. "My favorite!" After offering us a taste, which we declined, he took a large, noisy bite. I dismissed my assistant and watched as "prot" devoured the fruit. I had never seen anyone enjoy anything more. He ate every bit of both apples, including the seeds. When he had finished, he said, "Thanks and thanks," and waited for me to begin, his hands on his knees like a little boy's.

Although psychiatric interviews are not normally recorded, we do so routinely at MPI for research and teaching purposes. What follows is a transcript of that first session, interspersed with occasional observations on my part. As usual during initial interviews I planned simply to chat with the man, get to know him, gain his trust.

"Will you tell me your name, please?"

"Yes." Evidence for a sense of humor?

"What is your name?"

"My name is prot." He pronounced it to rhyme with "goat," not "hot."

"Is that your first name or your last?"

"That is all of my name. I am prot."

"Do you know where you are, Mr. prot?"

"Just prot. Yes, of course. I am in the manhattan psychiatric institute."

I discovered in due course that prot tended to capitalize the names of planets, stars, etc., but not those of persons, institutions, even countries. For the sake of consistency, and to better depict the character of my patient, I have adopted that convention throughout this report.

"Good. Do you know who I am?"

"You look like a psychiatrist."

"That's right. I'm Doctor Brewer. What day is it?"

"Ah. You're the acting director. Wednesday."

"Uh-huh. What year?"

"1990."

"How many fingers am I holding up?"

"Three."

"Very good. Now, Mr.—excuse me—prot: Do you know why you are here?"

"Of course. You think I'm crazy."

"I prefer to use the term 'ill.' Do you think you are ill?"

"A little homesick, perhaps."

"And where is 'home'?"

"K-PAX."

"Kaypacks?"

"Kay-hyphen-pee-ay-ex. K-PAX."

"With a capital kay?"

"It is all capitals."

"Oh. K-PAX. Is that an island?"

He smiled at this, apparently realizing I already knew he believed himself to be from another world. But he said, simply, "K-PAX is a PLANET." Then: "But don't worry—I'm not going to leap out of your chest."

I smiled back. "I wasn't worried. Where is K-PAX?"

He sighed, tolerantly it seemed, and shook his head. "About seven thousand light-years from here. It's in what you would call the CONSTELLATION LYRA."

"How did you get to Earth?"

"That's somewhat difficult to explain. . . ."

At this point I noted on my pad the surprising observation that, even though we had only been together a few minutes, and despite all my years of experience, I was becoming a little annoyed by the patient's obvious condescension. I said, "Try me."

"It's simply a matter of harnessing the energy of light. You may find this a little hard to believe, but it's done with mirrors."

I couldn't help feeling he was putting me on, but it was a good joke, and I suppressed a chuckle. "You travel at the speed of light?"

"Oh, no. We can travel many times that speed, various multiples of c. Otherwise, I'd have to be at least seven thousand years old, wouldn't I?"

I forced myself to return his smile. "That is very interesting," I said, "but according to Einstein nothing can travel faster than the speed of light, or one hundred and eighty-six thousand miles per second, if I remember correctly."

"You misunderstand einstein. What he said was that nothing can *accelerate* to the speed of light because its mass would become infinite. Einstein said nothing about entities *already* traveling at the speed of light, or faster."

"But if your mass becomes infinite when you—"

His feet plopped onto my desk. "In the first place, doctor brewer—may I call you gene?—if that were true, then photons themselves would have infinite mass, wouldn't they? And beyond that, at tachyon speeds—"

"Tachyon?"

"Entities traveling faster than the speed of light are called tachyons. You can look it up."

"Thank you. I will." My reply sounds a bit peevish on rehearing the tape. "If I understand you correctly, then, you did not come to Earth in a spaceship. You sort of 'hitched a ride' on a beam of light."

"You could call it that."

"How long did it take you to get to Earth from your planet?"

"No time at all. Tachyons, you see, travel faster than light and, therefore, backward in time. Time passes for the *traveler*, of course, and he becomes older than he was when he left."

"And how long have you been here on Earth?"

"Four years and nine months. *Your* years, that is."

"And that makes you how old now? In Earth terms, of course."

"Three hundred and thirty-seven."

"You are three hundred and thirty-seven years old?"

"Yes."

"All right. Please tell me a little more about yourself." Although I recognized the unreality of the man's story, it is standard psychiatric practice to draw out an amnesiacal patient in hopes of obtaining information about his true background.

"You mean before I came to EARTH? Or—"

"Let's start with this: How did you happen to be chosen to make the journey from your planet to ours?"

Now the patient was actually grinning at me. Though it seemed innocent enough, perhaps even ingenuous, I found myself poring through his file rather than gaze at his Cheshire-cat face in dark glasses. He said, " 'Chosen.' That's a peculiarly human concept." I looked up to find him scratching his chin and searching the ceiling in an apparent attempt to locate the appropriate words to explain his lofty thoughts to someone as lowly as myself. What he came up with was: "I wanted to come and I am here."

"Anyone who wants to come to Earth may do so?"

"Anyone on K-PAX. And a number of other PLAN-ETS, of course."

"Did anyone come with you?"

"No."

"Why did you want to come to Earth?"

"Pure curiosity. EARTH is a particularly lively place as seen and heard from space. And it is a Class III-B PLANET."

"Meaning . . . ?"

"Meaning early stage of evolution, future uncertain."

"I see. And is this your first trip to our planet?"

"Oh, no. I've been here many times."

"When was the first time?"

"In 1963, your calendar."

"And has anyone else from K-PAX visited us?"

"No. I am the first."

"I'm relieved to hear that."

"Why?"

"Let's just say it would cause a lot of people a certain amount of consternation."

"Why?"

"If you don't mind, I'd rather we talk about you today. Would that be all right?"

"If you wish."

"Good. Now—where else have you been? Around the universe, I mean."

"I have been to sixty-four PLANETS within our GAL-AXY."

"And on how many of those have you encountered life?"

"Why, on all of them. The ones that are barren don't interest me. Of course there are those who are fascinated by rocks and weather patterns and—"

"Sixty-four planets with intelligent life?"

"All life is intelligent."

"Well, how many have human beings such as our-selves?"

"EARTH is the only one with the species homo sapiens that I have visited so far. But we know there are a few others here and there."

"With intelligent life?"

"No, with human life. The PLANETS that support life number into the millions, possibly the billions. Of course we have not visited them all. That is only a rough estimate."

" 'We' meaning inhabitants of K-PAX."

"K-PAXians, NOLLians, FLORians . . ."

"Those are other races on your home planet?"

"No. They are inhabitants of other worlds." Most delu-sionals are confused to the point that they stutter or stumble considerably when trying to answer complex questions in a consistent manner. This patient was not only knowledgeable about a variety of arcane topics, but also confident enough of his knowledge to weave a cogent story. I scribbled on my pad the speculation that he might have been a scientist, perhaps a physicist or astronomer, and made a further note to determine how far his knowledge extended into those fields. For now, I wanted to learn something about his early life.

"Let's back up just a bit, if you don't mind. I'd like you to tell me something about K-PAX itself."

"Certainly. K-PAX is somewhat bigger than your PLANET, about the size of NEPTUNE. It is a beautiful world, as is EARTH, of course, with its color and variety. But K-PAX is also very lovely, especially when K-MON and K-RIL are in conjunction."

"What are K-MON and K-RIL?"

"Those are our two SUNS. What you call AGAPE and SATORI. One is much larger than yours, the other smaller, but both are farther from our PLANET than your SUN is from yours. K-MON is red and K-RIL blue. But owing to our larger and more complex orbital pattern, we have much longer periods of light and darkness than you do, and not so much variation. That is, most of the time on K-PAX it's something like your twilight. One of the things a visitor to your WORLD first notices is how bright it is here."

"Is that why you are wearing dark glasses?"

"Naturally."

"I'd like to clarify something you said earlier."

"Certainly."

"I believe you stated that you have been on Earth for four years and—uh—some odd months."

"Nine."

"Yes, nine. What I'd like very much to know is: Where were you living for those four or five years?"

"Everywhere."

"Everywhere?"

"I have traveled all over your WORLD."

"I see. And where did you begin your travels?"

"In zaire."

"Why Zaire? That's in Africa, isn't it?"

"It happened to be pointing toward K-PAX at the time."

"Ah. And how long were you there?"

"A couple of your weeks altogether. Long enough to become familiar with the land. Meet the beings there. All beautiful, especially the birds."

"Mm. Uh—what languages do they speak in Zaire?"

"You mean the humans, I presume."

"Yes."

"Besides the four official languages and french, there are an amazing number of native dialects."

"Can you say something in Zairese? Any dialect will do."

"Certainly. *Ma-ma kotta rampoon.*"

"What does that mean?"

"It means: Your mother is a gorilla."

"Thank you."

"No problem."

"And then where did you go? After Zaire."

"All over africa. Then to europe, asia, australia, antarctica, and finally to the americas."

"And how many countries have you visited?"

"All of them except eastern canada, greenland, and iceland. Those are my last stops."

"All—what—hundred of them?"

"More like two hundred at present, but it seems to change by the minute."

"And you speak all the languages?"

"Only enough to get by."

"How did you travel? Weren't you stopped at various borders?"

"I told you: It's difficult to explain. . . ."

"You mean you did it with mirrors."

"Exactly."

"How long does it take to go from country to country at the speed of light or whatever multiples of it you use?"

"No time at all."

"Does your father like to travel?" I detected a brief hesitation, but no strong reaction to the sudden mention of prot's father.

"I imagine. Most K-PAXians do."

"Well, *does* he travel? What kind of work does he do?"

"He does no work."

"What about your mother?"

"What about her?"

"Does she work?"

"Why should she?"

"They are both retired, then?"

"Retired from what?"

"From whatever they did for a living. How old are they?"

"Probably in their late six hundreds."

"Obviously they no longer work."

"Neither of them has ever worked." Apparently the patient considered his parents to be ne'er-do-wells, and the way he phrased his answer led me to believe that he harbored a deep-seated resentment or even hatred not only of his father (not uncommon) but of his mother (relatively rare for a man) as well. He continued: "No one 'works' on K-PAX. That is a human concept."

"No one does *anything*?"

"Of course not. But when you do something you want to do, it's not work, is it?" His grin widened. "You don't consider what you do to be work, do you?"

I ignored this smug comment. "We'll talk more about your parents later, all right?"

"Why not?"

"Fine. There are a couple of other things I'd like to clear up before we go on."

"Anything you say."

"Good. First, how do you account for the fact that, as a visitor from space, you look so much like an Earth person?"

"Why is a soap bubble round?"

"I don't know—why?"

"For an educated person, you don't know much, do you, gene? A soap bubble is round because that is the most energy-efficient configuration. Similarly, many beings around the UNIVERSE look pretty much like we do."

"I see. Okay, you mentioned earlier that—mm— 'EARTH is a particularly lively place as seen and heard from space.' What did you mean by that?"

"Your television and radio waves go out from EARTH in all directions. The whole GALAXY is watching and listening to everything you say and do."

"But these waves travel only at the speed of light, don't they? They couldn't possibly have reached K-PAX as yet."

He sighed again, more loudly this time. "But some of the energy goes into higher overtones, don'tcha know? It's this principle, in fact, that makes light travel possible. Have you studied physics?"

I suddenly remembered my long-suffering high school physics teacher, who had tried to drum this kind of information into my head. I also felt a need for a cigarette, though I hadn't smoked one in years. "I'll take your word for that, Mist—uh—prot. One more thing: Why do you travel around the universe all by yourself?"

"Wouldn't you, if you could?"

"Maybe. I don't know. But what I meant was: Why do you do it *alone?*"

14

"Is that why you think I'm crazy?"

"Not at all. But doesn't it get kind of lonely, all those years—four years and eight months, wasn't it?—in space?"

"No. And I wasn't in space that long. I've been *here* for four years and nine months."

"How long were you in space?"

"I aged about seven of your months, if that's what you mean."

"You didn't feel a need to have someone to talk to for all that time?"

"No." I jotted down: Patient dislikes *everyone?*

"What did you do to keep yourself occupied?"

He wagged his head. "You don't understand, gene. Although I became seven EARTH months older during the trip, it really seemed like an instant to me. You see, time is warped at super light speeds. In other words—"

Unforgivably, I was too annoyed to let him go on. "And speaking of time, ours is up for today. Shall we continue the discussion next week?"

"As you wish."

"Good. I'll call Mr. Kowalski and Mr. Jensen to escort you back to your ward."

"I know the way."

"Well, if you don't mind, I'd rather call them. Just routine hospital procedure. I'm sure you understand."

"Perfectly."

"Good." The orderlies arrived in a moment and the patient left with them, nodding complacently to me as he went out. I was surprised to find that I was dripping with perspiration, and I remember getting up to check the thermostat after switching off the recorder.

While the tape was rewinding I copied my scribbled observations for his permanent file, making mention of my distaste for what seemed to me his arrogant manner, after which I filed the rough notes into a separate cabinet, already stuffed with similar records. Then I listened to part of the tape, adding a comment about the patient's lack of any trace of dialect or accent. Surprisingly, hearing his soft voice, which was rather pleasant, was not at all annoying to me. It had been his demeanor. . . . Suddenly I realized: That cocky, lopsided, derisive grin reminded me of my father.

DAD was an overworked small-town doctor. The only time he ever relaxed—except for Saturday afternoons, when he lay on the sofa with his eyes closed listening to the Metropolitan Opera broadcasts—was at dinnertime, when he would have exactly one glass of wine and relate to my mother and me, in his offhand way, more than we wanted to know about the ringworms and infarctions of his day. Afterwards he would head back to the hospital or make a few house calls. Unless I could think up a good excuse he would take me with him, assuming, erroneously, that I enjoyed the noxious sounds and smells, the bleeding and vomiting as much as he did. It was that insensitivity and arrogance, which I hated in my father, that had annoyed me so much during my first encounter with this man who called himself "prot."

I resolved, as always when something like this happens, to keep my personal life out of the examining room.

ON the train home that evening I got to thinking, as I often do after beginning a difficult or unusual case, about the human mind and reality. My new patient, for example, and Russell, our resident Christ, and thousands like them live in worlds of their own, realms just as real to them as yours and mine are to us. That seems difficult to understand, but is it really? Surely the reader of this account has become, at one time or another, thoroughly involved in a film or absorbed in a novel, utterly "lost" in the experience. Dreams, even daydreams, often seem very real at the time, as do events recalled during hypnosis. On such occasions, who is to say what reality is?

It is quite remarkable what some of those with severe mental disorders are able to do within the boundaries of their illusory worlds. The "idiot" savants are a case in point. Unable to function in our society, they withdraw into recesses of the mind which most of us can never enter. They are capable of feats—with numbers, for example, or music—that others cannot begin to duplicate. We are still in the Dark Ages as far as understanding the human mind is concerned—how it learns, how it remembers, how it *thinks*. If Einstein's brain were transplanted into Wagner's skull, would this individual still be Einstein? Better: Switch half of Einstein's brain with half of Wagner's—which person would be Einstein and which Wagner? Or would each be someone in between? Similarly, in the case of multiple personality syndrome, which of the distinct "identities" is really the person in question, or is he/she a *different* person at different times? Are we *all* different people at different times? Could this explain our changing "moods"? When we see someone talking to himself—to whom is he speaking? Have you ever heard someone say, "I haven't been myself lately."? Or "You're not the man I married!"? And how do we account for the fundamentalist preacher and his clandestine sex life? Are we all Drs. Jekyll and Messrs. Hyde?

I made a note to dwell for a while on prot's imaginary life on his imaginary planet, hoping of course that this would reveal something about his background on Earth—his geographical origin, perhaps, his occupation, his name!—so that we might be able to track down his family and friends and thus, in addition to allaying their fears about his health and whereabouts, get to the underlying cause for his bizarre confabulation. I was beginning to feel the little tingle I always get at the beginning of a challenging case, when all the possibilities are still open. Who was this man? What sorts of alien thoughts filled his head? Would we be able to bring him down to Earth?

Session Two

I have always tried to give my examining room as pleasant an atmosphere as possible, with cheerful pastel walls, a few sylvan watercolors, and soft, indirect lighting. There is no couch: My patient and I sit facing each other in comfortable chairs. There is a clock placed discreetly on the back wall where the patient cannot see it.

Before my second interview with prot I went over Joyce Trexler's transcript of the first week's session with him. Mrs. Trexler has been here almost forever and it is common knowledge that it is she who really runs the place. "Crazy as a loon" was her uninvited comment as she dropped the typed copy onto my desk.

I had looked up "tachyons" and found that they were, as he had indicated, entities traveling faster than light. They are purely theoretical, however, and there is no evidence suggesting their actual existence. I had also tried to check out the "Zairese," but couldn't find anyone who spoke any of its more than two hundred dialects. However, although his story seemed perfectly consistent, it was no less problematic.

In psychoanalysis, one tries to become the patient's peer. Gain his confidence. Build on what grasp he still has of reality, his residue of normal thoughts. But this man had *no* grasp of reality. His alleged travels around the world offered some sort of earthbound experience to pursue, but even that was suspect—he could have spent time in the library, or watched travelogues, for example. I was still pondering how to gain some kind of toehold on prot's psyche when he was escorted into my examining room.

He was wearing the same blue corduroys, dark glasses, and familiar smile. But this time the latter did not annoy me so much—it had been my problem, not his. He requested a few bananas before we began, and offered one to me. I declined, and waited until he had devoured them, skins and all. "Your produce alone," he said, "has made the trip worthwhile."

We chatted for a few minutes about fruit. He reminded me, for example, that their characteristic odors and flavors are due to the presence of specific chemical compounds known as esters. Then we reviewed briefly our previous interview. He maintained that he had arrived on Earth some four years and nine months ago, traveled on a beam of light, etc. Now I learned that "K-PAX" was circled by seven purple moons. "Your planet must be a very romantic place," I prodded. At this point he did a surprising thing, something that no other patient of mine has ever done in the nearly thirty years I have been practicing psychoanalysis: He pulled a pencil and a little red notebook from his shirt pocket and began taking notes of his own! Rather amused by this, I asked him what he was jotting down. He replied that he had thought of something to include in his report. I inquired as to the nature of this "report." He said it was his custom to compile a description of the various places he visited and beings he encountered throughout the galaxy. It appeared that the patient was examining the doctor! It was my turn to smile.

Not wanting to inhibit his activities in any way, I did not press him to show me what he had written, though I was more than a little curious. Instead, I asked him to tell me something about his boyhood on "K-PAX" (i.e., Earth).

He said, "The region I was born in—incidentally, we are *born* on K-PAX, just like you, and the process is much the same, only—well, we'll get into that later, I suppose. . . ."

"Why don't we go into it now?"

He paused briefly, as if taken aback, but quickly recovered. The little grin, however, was gone. "If you wish. Our anatomy is much like yours, as you know from the physical examination. The physiology is also similar, but, unlike on EARTH, the reproduction process is quite unpleasant."

"What makes it unpleasant?"

"It is a very painful procedure."

Ah, I thought, a breakthrough: Mr. "prot" very possibly suffers some sort of sexual terror or dysfunction. I quickly pursued this lead. "Is this pain associated with intercourse itself, with ejaculation, or merely with obtaining an erection?"

"It is associated with the entire process. Where these activities result in pleasurable sensations for beings such as yourself, for us the effect is quite the opposite. This applies both to the males and females of our species and, incidentally, to most other beings around the GALAXY as well."

"Can you compare the sensation to anything else I might be able to understand or identify with? Is it like a toothache, or—"

"It's more like having your gonads caught in a vise, except that we feel it all over. You see, on K-PAX pain is more general, and to make matters worse it is associated with something like your nausea, accompanied by a very bad smell. The moment of climax is like being kicked in the stomach and falling into a pool of *mot* shit."

"Did you say *mot* shit? What is a 'mot'?"

"An animal something like your skunk, only far more potent."

"I see." Unforgivably I began to laugh. This image coupled with the dark glasses and suddenly serious demeanor—well, as they say, you had to be there. He grinned broadly then, apparently understanding how it must have sounded to me. I managed to regain my composure and carry on. "And you say it is the same for a woman?"

"Exactly the same. As you can imagine, women on K-PAX do not strive very hard to reach orgasm."

"If the experience is so terrible, how do you reproduce?"

"Like your porcupines: as carefully as possible. Needless to say, overpopulation is not a problem for us."

"What about something like surgical implantation?"

"You are distorting the importance of the phenomenon. You have to bear in mind that since the life span for our species is a thousand of your years, there is little need to produce children."

"I see. All right. I'd like to get back to your own childhood. Can you tell me a little about your upbringing? What were your parents like?"

"That's a little difficult to explain. Life on K-PAX is quite different from that on EARTH. In order for you to understand my background, I will have to tell you something about our evolution." He paused at this point, as if wondering whether I would be interested in hearing what he had to say. I encouraged him to proceed. "Well, I suppose the best place to start is at the beginning. Life on K-PAX is much older than life on EARTH, which began about two-point-five billion years ago. Homo sapiens has existed on your PLANET for only a few tens of thousands of years, give or take a millennium or two. On K-PAX, life began nearly nine billion of your years ago, when your WORLD was still a diffuse ball of gas. Our own species has been around for five billion of those years, considerably longer than your bacteria. Furthermore, evolution took a quite different course. You see, we have very little water on our PLANET, compared to EARTH—no oceans at all, no rivers, no lakes—so life began on land or, more precisely, underground. Your species evolved from the fishes; our forefathers were something like your worms."

"And yet you evolved into something very much like us."

"I thought I explained that in our previous discussion. You could check your notes. . . ."

"This is all very interesting—uh—prot, but what does paleontology have to do with your upbringing?"

"Everything—just as it does on EARTH."

"Why don't we proceed with your childhood, and we can come back to this relationship later if I have any questions about it. Would that be all right?"

He bent over the notebook again. "Certainly."

"Very well. First, let's talk about some of the fundamental items, shall we? For example, how often do you see your parents? Are your grandparents still alive? Do you have any brothers or sisters?"

"Gene, gene, gene. You haven't been listening. Things are not the same on K-PAX as they are on EARTH. We don't have 'families' as you know the term. The whole idea of a 'family' would be a non sequitur on our PLANET, and on most others. Children are not raised by their biological parents, but by everyone. They circulate among us, learning from one, then another."

"Would it be fair to say, then, that as a child you had no home to go to?"

"Exactly. Now you've got it."

"In other words you never knew your parents."

"I had thousands of parents."

I made a note that prot's denying his father and mother confirmed my earlier suspicion of a deep-seated hatred of one or both, possibly due to abuse, or perhaps he had been orphaned, or neglected, or even abandoned by them. "Would you say you had a happy childhood?"

"Very."

"Can you think of any unpleasant experiences you had as a child?"

Prot's eyes closed tightly, as they often did when he tried to concentrate or to recollect something. "Not really. Nothing unusual. I was knocked down by an ap a couple of times, and squirted by a mot once or twice. And I had something like your measles and mumps. Little things like that."

"An 'ap'?"

"Like a small elephant."

"Where was this?"

"On K-PAX."

"Yes, but where on K-PAX? Your own country?"

"We don't have countries on K-PAX."

"Well, do elephants run around loose there?"

"Everything runs around loose there. We don't have zoos."

"Are any of the animals dangerous?"

"Only if you get in their way."

24

"Do you have a wife waiting for you back on K-PAX?" This was another toss from left field, again to determine the effect of a key word on the patient's state of mind. Except for a barely perceptible shift in his chair, he remained calm.

"We don't *have* marriage on K-PAX—no husbands, no wives, no families—get it? Or, to put it more correctly, the entire population is one big family."

"Do you have any biological children of your own?"

"No."

There are many reasons why a person decides not to have children. One of these has to do with abuse by or hatred of his parents. "Let's get back to your mother and father. Do you see them very often?"

He sighed in apparent frustration. "No."

"Do you like them?"

"Are you still beating your wife?"

"I don't understand."

"Your questions are phrased from the point of view of an EARTH person. On K-PAX they would be nonsense."

"Mr. prot—"

"Just prot."

"Let's establish some sort of ground rules for these sessions, shall we? I'm sure you will forgive me if I phrase my questions from the point of view of an Earth person since, in fact, that is what I am. I could not phrase them in K-PAXian terms even if I wanted to because I am not familiar with your way of life. I am going to ask you to humor me, to bear with me in this. Please try to answer the questions in the best way you can, using Earth expressions, which you seem to be quite familiar with, whenever possible. Would that be a fair request under the circumstances?"

"I am happy you have said that. Perhaps we can learn from each other."

"If you are happy, I am happy too. Now, if you are ready, maybe you could tell me a little about your parents. For example, do you know who your mother and father are? Have you ever met them?"

"I have met my mother. I have not yet run across my father."

It's his father the patient hates! " 'Run across'?"

"K-PAX is a big place."

"But surely—"

"Or if I have met him, no one has pointed out our biological relationship."

"Are there many people on your planet who don't know who their fathers are?"

He grinned at this, quickly picking up on the double meaning. "Most do not. It is not an important thing."

"But you know your mother."

"Purely a coincidence. A mutual acquaintance happened to mention our biological connection."

"That is difficult for an Earth person to understand. Perhaps you could explain why your 'biological connections' are not important to you."

"Why should they be?"

"Because—uh, for now, let me ask the questions, and you give the answers, all right?"

"Sometimes a question is the best answer."

"I suppose you don't know how many brothers and sisters you have."

"On K-PAX we are all siblings."

"I meant biological siblings."

"I would be surprised if there were any. Almost no one has more than one child, for reasons I have already explained."

"Isn't there peer pressure or government incentives to make sure your species doesn't die out?"

"There is no government on K-PAX."

"What do you mean—it's an anarchy?"

"That's as good a word as any."

"But who builds the roads? The hospitals? Who runs the schools?"

"Really, gene, it's not that difficult to understand. On K-PAX, one does what needs to be done."

"What if no one notices that something needs to be done? What if someone knows something needs to be done but refuses to do it? What if a person decides to do nothing?"

"That doesn't happen on K-PAX."

"Never?"

"What would be the point?"

"Well, to express dissatisfaction over the wages being paid, for one thing."

"We don't have 'wages' on K-PAX. Or money of any kind."

I jotted this down. "No money? What do you barter with?"

"We don't 'barter.' You really should learn to listen to your patients, doctor. I told you before—if something needs to be done, you do it. If someone needs something you have, you give it to him. This avoids a multitude of problems and has worked pretty well on our PLANET for several billion years."

"All right. How big is your planet?"

"About the size of your NEPTUNE. You'll find this also on the transcript of last week's conversation."

"Thank you. And what is the population?"

"There are about fifteen million of my species, if that is

what you mean. But there are many other beings besides ourselves."

"What kinds of beings?"

"A variety of creatures, some of whom resemble the animals of EARTH, some not."

"Are these wild or domesticated animals?"

"We don't 'domesticate' any of our beings."

"You don't raise any animals for food?"

"No one 'raises' another being for any purpose on K-PAX, and certainly not for food. We are not cannibals." I detected a sudden and unexpected note of anger in this response—why?

"Let me just fill in one or two blanks in your childhood. As I understand it, you were brought up by a number of surrogate parents, is that right?"

"Not exactly."

"Well, who took care of you? Tucked you into bed at night?"

Utterly exasperated: "No one 'tucks you into bed' on K-PAX. When you are sleepy, you sleep. When you are hungry, you eat."

"Who feeds you?"

"No one. Food is always around."

"At what age did you begin school?"

"There are no schools on K-PAX."

"I'm not surprised. But you are obviously an educated person."

"I am not a 'person.' I am a being. All K-PAXians are educated. But education does not come from schools. Education stems from the desire to learn. With that, you don't need schools. Without it, all the schools in the UNIVERSE are useless."

"But how did you learn? Are there teachers?"

"On K-PAX, everyone is a teacher. If you have a question, you just ask whoever is around. And of course there are the libraries."

"Libraries? Who runs the libraries?"

"Gene, gene, gene. No one does. Everyone does."

"Are these libraries structures we Earth people would recognize?"

"Probably. There are books there. But many other things as well. Things you would not recognize or understand."

"Where are these libraries? Does each city have one?"

"Yes, but our 'cities' are more like what you would call 'villages.' We have no vast metropolises such as the one in which we are presently located."

"Does K-PAX have a capital?"

"No."

"How do you get from one village to another? Are there trains? Cars? Airplanes?"

A deep sigh was followed by some incoherent mumbling in a language I couldn't understand (later identified as "pax-o"). He made another entry in his notebook. "I have explained this before, gino. We get from place to place on the energy of light. Why do you find this concept so hard to understand? Is it too simple for you?"

We had been over this before and, with time running out, I did not intend to be sidetracked again. "One final question. You have said that your childhood was a happy one. Did you have other children to play with?"

"Hardly any. There are very few children anywhere on K-PAX, as I have indicated. Besides that, there is no distinction between 'work' and 'play' on our PLANET. On

EARTH, children are encouraged to play all the time. This is because you believe they should remain innocent of their approaching adulthood for as long as possible, apparently because the latter is so distasteful. On K-PAX, children and adults are all part of the same thing. On our PLANET life is fun, and interesting. There is no need for mindless games, either for children or adults. No need for escape into soap operas, football, alcohol, or other drugs. Did I have a happy childhood on K-PAX? Of course. And a happy adulthood as well."

I didn't know whether to feel gladdened or saddened by this cheerful answer. On the one hand, the man seemed genuinely content with his imaginary lot. On the other, it was obvious he was denying not only his family, but his school experiences, his childhood itself. Even his country. Everything. Every aspect of his entire life, which must have been quite abominable, indeed. I felt a great deal of pity for this young man.

I ended the interview with a question about his "home town," but this also led nowhere. K-PAXians seemed to drift from place to place like nomads.

I dismissed the patient and he returned to his ward. I had been so astonished by his utter denial of everything human that I forgot to call the orderlies to go with him.

After he had gone I returned to my adjacent office and went through his entire file again. I had never experienced a case like this, one for which I couldn't seem to find any kind of handle. Only one other in thirty years was even close, and it also involved an amnesiac. A student of mine was eventually able to trace the man's roots through an analysis of his reawakened interest in sports—but it took a couple of years.

I jotted down what I had on prot so far:

1. P hates his parents—had he been abused?
2. P hates his job, the government, perhaps society as a
   whole—had there been a legal problem resulting in a
   perceived injustice?
3. Did something happen 4–5 yrs ago that underlay all these
   apparent hatreds?
4. On top of everything else, the patient has a severe sex
   hangup.

As I looked over these notes I remembered something
that my colleague Klaus Villers has professed on more than
one occasion: Extraordinary cases require extraordinary measures. I was thinking of the rare instances in which a delusional of exceptional intelligence has been convinced that his
identity was false. The most famous example of this treatment
is the one in which a well-known comedian graciously con-
sented to confront a delusional look-alike, and a miraculous
cure was quickly effected (but not before they both put on
quite a show, evidently). If I could prove to prot that he was,
in fact, an ordinary human being and not some alien from
another planet . . .

I decided to do a more thorough physical and mental
workup on him. I was particularly interested in learning
whether he was, in fact, abnormally sensitive to light, as he
claimed to be. I also wanted to have the results of an aptitude
test and to determine the extent of his general knowledge,
particularly in the areas of physics and astronomy. The more
we knew about his background, the easier it would be to find
out who he really was.

WHEN I was a senior in high school our career counselor
advised me to take the one course in physics our school of-

fered. I quickly learned that I had no aptitude for the subject, though the experience did serve to increase my respect for anyone who could master that esoteric material, among them my wife-to-be.

We were next-door neighbors from the day she was born, Karen and I, and we played together all the time. Every morning I would go outside and find her in the yard, smiling and ready for anything. One of the fondest memories I have is of our first day in school, of sitting behind her where I could smell her hair, of walking home with her and leaves burning. Of course we weren't really sweethearts at that age—not until we were twelve, the year my father died.

It happened in the middle of the night. My mother came and got me up because she hoped, vainly as it turned out, that I might be able to do something. When I ran into their bedroom I found him lying on his back, naked, sweating, his pajamas on the floor beside the bed. He was still breathing, but his face was ashen. I had spent enough time in his office and on hospital rounds to suspect what had happened and to recognize the seriousness of the situation. If he had taught me something about closed-chest massage I might have been able to help him, but this was before CPR was generally known and there was nothing I could do except watch him gasp his last breath and expire. Of course I yelled at my mother to call an ambulance, but it was far too late by the time it got there. In the meantime I studied his body with horrible fascination, his graying hands and feet, his knobby knees, his large, dark genitalia. Mother came running back just as I was covering him with the sheet. There was no need to tell her. She knew. Oh, she knew.

Afterwards, I found myself in a state of profound shock and confusion. Not because I loved him, but because I didn't—had almost wished him dead, in fact, so I wouldn't have to become a doctor like him. Ironically, because of the tremendous sense of guilt I felt, I vowed to go into medicine anyway.

At the funeral, Karen, without anyone saying anything, sat beside me and held my hand. It was as though she understood perfectly what I was going through. I squeezed hers too, hard. It was unbelievably soft and warm. I didn't feel any less guilty, but with her hand in mine it seemed as though I might be able to get through life somehow. And I've been holding it ever since.

ON Friday of that week we received a visitor from the State Board of Health. His job is to check our facilities periodically, see that the patients are clean and properly fed, that the plumbing works, etc. Although he had been here many times before, we gave him the usual grand tour: the kitchen, the dining and laundry and furnace rooms, the shop, the grounds, the recreation/exercise room, the quiet room, the medical facilities, and, finally, the wards.

It was in the rec room that we found prot sitting at a card table with two of my other patients. I thought that a bit odd inasmuch as one of them, whom I shall call Ernie, almost always keeps to himself, or talks quietly with Russell, our unofficial chaplain. The other, Howie, is usually too busy to talk to anyone (the white rabbit syndrome). Both Ernie and Howie have been here for years, sharing the same room, and both are very difficult cases.

Ernie, like most people, is afraid of death. Unlike most of us, however, he is unable to think about anything else. He checks his pulse and temperature regularly. He insists on wearing a surgical mask and rubber gloves at all times. He is never without his stethoscope and thermometer and he showers several times a day, demanding fresh clothing after each one, rejecting anything that shows the slightest spot or stain. We humor him in this because otherwise he would wear nothing.

Eating is a serious problem for Ernie, for several reasons. First, because of his fear of food poisoning he will not consume anything that isn't thoroughly cooked and comes to him piping hot. Second, he will only eat food that is broken or cut into tiny pieces so he won't choke to death on something too large to swallow. Finally, there is the problem of preservatives and additives. He will not eat meat or poultry, and is suspicious even of fresh fruits and vegetables.

None of this is unusual, of course, and every psychiatric hospital has an Ernie or two. What makes Ernie different is that he raises his defenses a notch or two higher than most necrophobes. He cannot be induced to venture outside the building, for example, fearing bombardment by meteorites, cosmic rays and the like, poisoning by chemicals in the air, attack by insects and birds, infection by dust-borne organisms, and so on.

But that's not all. Afraid he will unconsciously strangle himself at night he sleeps with his hands tied to his feet, and bites down on a wooden dowel so he won't swallow his tongue. For similar reasons he will not lie under sheets or blankets—he fears they might wrap themselves around his throat—and he sleeps on the floor so as not to fall out of bed and break his neck. As a sort of compensation, perhaps, he sleeps quite soundly once his ritual is complete, though he awakens early to fitfully check his parameters and accouterments, and by the time he has breakfast is his usual nervous wreck.

How could a person get so screwed up? When Ernie was a boy of nine he watched his mother choke to death on a piece of meat. Unable to help, he was condemned to witness her last agonizing moments while his older sister ran around the kitchen, screaming. Before he could get over that horrible experience, his father dug a bomb shelter in the back yard and practiced using it. Here's how it worked: At any moment of the day or night Ernie's father would suddenly leap at him or emit a blood-curdling screech or douse him with something. That would be the signal to run for the bomb shelter. By the time he was eleven Ernie was unable to speak or to stop shaking. When he was brought to MPI it took months just to get him not to jump and run whenever a door opened or someone sneezed. That was nearly twenty years ago, and he has been here ever since. His father, incidentally, is a patient at another institution; his sister committed suicide in 1980.

Fortunately, debilitating phobias like Ernie's are rare. Those who are afraid of snakes, for example, need only stay away from forest and field. Agoraphobics and claustrophobics can usually avoid crowds and elevators and, in any case, are treatable with drugs or by slow acclimation to the offending situation. But how does one acclimate the necrophobic? How to avoid the Grim Reaper?

Howie is forty-three, though he looks to be sixty. Born into a poor Brooklyn family, his musical abilities became evident early on. His father gave him his unused violin when he was four years old and, in his early teens, he played that instrument with a number of well-respected regional orchestras. As time went on, however, he performed less and less frequently, preferring instead to study scores, other instruments, the history of music. His father, a bookseller, was not particularly concerned with this turn of events and went about his tiny shop bragging that Howie was going to become a famous conductor, another Stokowski. But by the time Howie got to college his interests seemed to cover the entire spectrum of human endeavor. He tried to master everything from algebra to Zen. He studied night and day until he finally broke down and ended up with us.

As soon as his physical health was restored, however, he was off and running again, and no tranquilizing drug has proven powerful enough to slow down his endless quest for perfection.

The strain on Howie is terrible. The circles and bags under his eyes attest to his chronic battle with fatigue, and he suffers constantly from colds and other minor afflictions.

What happened to him? Why does one artist end up at Carnegie Hall and another in a mental hospital? Howie's father was a very demanding man, intolerant of mistakes. When little Howie stood up to play the violin he was terrified of making the slightest false note and offending his father, whom he loved deeply. But the better he became the more he realized how much he did *not* know, and how much more room for error there was than he had imagined. In order to be certain of playing his instrument perfectly he threw himself into music in all its aspects, trying to learn everything about the subject. When he realized that even this would not be sufficient, he took up other fields of study with the impossible goal of learning everything there was to know about everything.

But even that isn't enough for Howie, who spends each summer cataloging the birds and insects and counting the blades of grass on the lawn outside. In the winter he catches snowflakes, systematically recording and comparing their structures. On clear nights he scans the skies looking for anomalies, something that wasn't there before. Yet these are mere avocations for Howie. Most of the time he reads dictionaries and encyclopedias while listening to music or language tapes. Afraid he will forget something important he is constantly taking notes and making lists, then organizing and re-organizing them. Until that day in the recreation room I had never seen him when he was not frantically counting, record-ing, or studying. It was a struggle to get him to take time to eat.

I edged up to the table with my guest, trying to catch a bit of the conversation without scaring anyone off. From what I could gather, they were querying prot about life on K-PAX. They clammed up when they finally noticed us, however, and both Ernie and Howie scuttled away.

I introduced prot to our visitor, and took the opportu-nity to ask him whether he would mind submitting to a few additional tests on Wednesday, our regular meeting day. He not only didn't mind, he said, but he looked forward to it. We left him smiling broadly, apparently in eager anticipation.

ALTHOUGH we would not receive the official report from the State Board of Health for several months, the representa-tive did point out two or three minor deficiencies that needed to be corrected, and I brought these up at the regular Monday morning staff meeting. Among the other items discussed at that meeting was the news that the search committee had nar-rowed down their list of possible candidates for permanent director to four—three from outside the hospital, and myself. The chair of that committee was Dr. Klaus Villers.

Villers is the kind of psychiatrist usually portrayed in films: sixtyish, pale, trim gray goatee, heavy German accent, and a strict Freudian. It was clear that he had selected the other three names personally. I was familiar with their work and each, on paper, was a reasonable facsimile of Villers him-self. But all had outstanding credentials, and I was looking forward to meeting them. My own candidacy was not unexpected, but I had mixed feelings about the directorship—it would have meant permanently giving up most of my patients, among other things.

When that business was taken care of I summarized for my colleagues what I had learned so far about prot. Villers and some of the others agreed that it would be a waste of time to proceed with ordinary psychoanalysis, but thought my attempt to "humanize" him would also prove fruitless, suggesting instead some of the newer experimental drugs. Others argued that this approach was premature and, in any case, without the consent of the patient's family, the legal ramifications could become complicated. Thus, it was generally agreed that a greater effort should be made, by the police as well as myself, to determine his true identity. I thought of Meyerbeer's opera *L'Africaine*, in which Inez awaits the return of her long-departed lover, Vasco da Gama, and I wondered: Was there a family somewhere in this wide world fervently hoping and praying for a missing husband and father, brother or son to reappear?

Session Three

T H E testing took all morning and half the afternoon of May twenty-third. I had other pressing duties much of that time, not the least of which was an emergency facilities committee meeting to approve the purchase of a new linen dryer for the laundry room following the irreversible breakdown of one of the two old ones. Betty McAllister served very well in my place, however.

At the time, Betty had been with us for eleven years, the last two in the capacity of head nurse. She was the only person I had ever met who had read all of Taylor Caldwell's novels and, as long as I had known her, had been trying to get pregnant. Although she had resorted to almost every known scientific and folk remedy, she eschewed the so-called fertility pills because, as she put it, "I only want the one, not a whole menagerie." None of this affected her work, however, and she consistently performed her duties cheerfully and well.

According to Betty's report, prot was extremely cooperative throughout the examination period. Indeed, the eagerness with which he attacked the tests and questionnaires supported my earlier speculation of an academic background. How far he had progressed with his education was still a matter of conjecture, but it seemed quite likely, based on his confident demeanor and general articulateness, that he had at least attended college and possibly even a graduate or professional school.

It took a few days to process the data, and I must confess that my curiosity was such that I let lapse some things I had planned to do at home in order to come in on Saturday to finish what Betty had not completed by Friday afternoon. The final results, though generally unremarkable (as I had expected), were nonetheless interesting. They are summarized as follows:

IQ	154 *(well above average, though not in genius category)*
Psychological tests *(left/right, mazes, mirror tests, etc.—addnl. to std. admission exam)*	normal
Neurological tests	normal
EEG *(performed by Dr. Chakraborty)*	normal
Short-term memory	excellent
Reading skill	very good
Artistic ability/eidetic imagery	variable
Musical ability	below average

General knowledge *(history, geography, languages, the arts)*	broad and impressive
Math and science *(particularly physics and astronomy)*	outstanding
Knowledge of sports	minimal
General physical strength	above average
Hearing, taste, smell, tactile acuities	highly sensitive
"Special senses" *(ability to "feel" colors, sense the presence of other people, etc.)*	questionable
Vision 1. Sensitivity to white light 2. Range	marked! can detect light at 300–400 Å (UV)!
Aptitude	could do almost anything; particular affinity for natural history and physical sciences

As can be seen, the only unusual finding was the patient's ability to see light at wavelengths well into the ultraviolet range. His apparent sensitivity to visible light could have been due to a genetic defect; in any case there was no obvious retinal damage (nevertheless, I made a note to call Dr. Rappaport, our ophthalmologist, first thing on Tuesday, Monday being Memorial Day). Otherwise there was no suggestion of any special alien talents.

The patient's knowledge of languages, incidentally, was

not as broad as he pretended. Although he spoke and read a little of most of the common ones, his understanding was limited to everyday phrases and idioms, the types found in books for travelers. Another thing that caught my eye was some information the patient volunteered about the stars in the constellation Lyra—their distances from Earth, types, etc.—nothing that required space travel to obtain, certainly, but I decided to check this out as well.

Driving home that afternoon to the accompaniment of Gounod's *Faust*, I marveled once again, as I bellowed along, at what the human mind can do. There are well-documented cases of superhuman strength arising from a desperate need or fit of madness, of astounding performances far beyond the normal capabilities of athletes or rescue workers, of people who can go into trancelike states or "hibernation," of extraordinary endurance exhibited by victims of natural or man-made disasters, accounts of paralyzed people who get up and walk, of cancer patients who almost seem to cure themselves or, by force of will alone, manage to hang on until a birthday or favorite holiday. No less striking, perhaps, is the case of the unattractive woman who comes across as beautiful merely because she thinks she is. An individual with little talent who becomes a Broadway star on the basis of self-confidence and energy alone. I have personally encountered many patients who have done amazing things they could not do before they became ill. And here we have a man who believes he comes from a planet where people are a little more light-sensitive than we are, and by God he is. At times like these one wonders what the limits of the human mind really are.

O N Memorial Day my oldest daughter and her husband and their two little boys drove up from Princeton for a cookout. Abigail is the reverse of the unattractive woman I mentioned above—she was always a very pretty girl who never realized it. I don't think she has ever used makeup, doesn't do anything with her hair, pays no attention to what she wears. From the beginning she has had a mind of her own. When I think of Abby I see a kid of eight or nine marching with a bunch of others two or three times her age, all with long hair and flared pants, flashing her peace sign and yelling her slogans, serious as a kiss. Now, as a nonpracticing lawyer, she's active in any number of women's/gay/environmental/civil/animal rights groups. How did she turn out this way? Who knows? All of our children are as different from each other as the colors of the rainbow.

Fred, for instance, is the most sensitive of the four. As a boy he always had his nose in a book, and an ear for music as well. In fact, he still has an enormous collection of recordings of Broadway shows. We always thought he would become an artist of some kind, and were quite amazed when he ended up in aeronautics.

Jennifer is very different still. Slim, beautiful, not as serious as Abigail or as quiet as Fred, she is the only one of the four who has shown any interest in following her old man's footsteps. As a girl she loved biology (and slumber parties and chocolate-chip cookies), and she is now a third-year medical student at Stanford.

Will (Chip) is the youngest, eight years younger than Jenny. Probably the brightest of the bunch, he is a star athlete in school, active, popular. Like Abby before him, and unlike Fred and Jenny, he is hardly ever home, preferring instead to spend his time with his friends rather than with his grizzled parents. He hasn't the foggiest idea what he wants to do with his life.

All of which leads to the question: Is the shape of the individual personality due primarily to genetic or to environmental factors? After a great deal of experimentation and debate on this critical issue, the answer is far from clear. All I know is that, despite similar backgrounds and genetic makeup, my four kids are as different from each other as is night from day, winter from summer.

Abby's husband Steve is a professor of astronomy and, while the steaks were sizzling on the grill, I mentioned to him that there was a patient at the hospital who seemed to know something about his field. I showed him prot's figures on the constellation Lyra and the double star system Agape and Satori, around which traveled a putative planet the patient called "K-PAX." Steve studied the information, scratched his reddish beard, and grunted, as he often does when he is thinking. Suddenly he looked up with a ferocious grin and drawled, "Charlie put you up to this, didn' he?"

I assured him that he hadn't, that I didn't even know who "Charlie" was.

He said, "Terrific joke. Ah love it." My grandson Rain was banging him with a Frisbee now, trying to get him to play, after failing to coax Shasta Daisy, our neurotic Dalmatian, out from under the porch.

I told him it was no joke and asked him why he thought so. I don't recall his exact words, but they went something like: "This is somethin' Charlie Flynn and his students have been workin' on for quite a while. It involves a double star in the constellation Lyra. This double shows certain perturbations in its rotation pattern that indicate the possibility of a large dark body, prob'ly a planet, as part of the system. Like your alleged patient said, this planet appears to travel around them in an unusual pattern—Charlie thinks it's a figure eight. Do you see what Ah'm sayin'? This is unpublished work! Except for one or two colleagues, Charlie hasn't told anybody about this yet; he was plannin' to report it at the Astrophysics

44

meeting next month. Where does this 'patient' of yours come from? How long has he been at the hospital? His name id'n 'Charlie,' is it?" He stuffed his mouth with a handful of potato chips.

We drank beer and chatted about astronomy and psychiatry most of the afternoon, Abby and her mother nagging us not to talk shop and to pay some attention to our sons/grandsons, who kept throwing food at Shasta and each other. One thing I wanted to know was his opinion on the possibility of light travel. "It's not," he stated flatly, still not convinced, I think, that I wasn't pulling his leg. But when I asked if he would be willing to help me prove to my new patient that "K-PAX" was a figment of his imagination, he said, "Shore." Before they left I gave him a list of questions to ask Dr. Flynn about the double star system—the types of stars they were, their actual sizes and brightnesses, their rotation period, the duration of a "year" on the putative planet, even something about what the night sky would look like from such a world. He promised to call me with whatever information he could dig up.

Session Four

T H E Manhattan Psychiatric Institute is located on Amsterdam Avenue at 112th Street in New York City. It is a private teaching and research hospital affiliated with the nearby Columbia University College of Physicians and Surgeons. MPI is distinct from the Psychiatric Institute at Columbia, which is a general treatment center that deals with far more patients. We refer to it as "the big institute," and ours, in turn, is known as "the little institute." Our concept is unique: We take in only a limited number of adult patients (one hundred to one hundred twenty in all), either cases of unusual interest or those that have proven unresponsive to standard somatic (drug), electroconvulsive, surgical, or psychotherapies.

MPI was constructed in 1907 at a cost of just over a million dollars. Today the physical facility alone is worth one hundred fifty million. The grounds, though small, are well kept, with a grassy lawn to the side and back, and shrubs and flower gardens along the walls and fences. There is also a fountain, "Adonis in the Garden of Eden," situated in the center of what we call "the back forty." I love to stroll these pastoral grounds, listen to the bubbly fountain, contemplate the old stone walls. Entire adult lives have been lived here, both patient and staff. To some, this is the only world they will ever know.

There are five floors at MPI, numbered essentially in order of increasing severity of patient illness. Ward One (ground floor) is for those who suffer only acute neuroses or mild paranoia, and those who have responded to therapy and are nearly ready to be discharged. The other patients know this and often try very hard to be "promoted" to Ward One. Ward Two is occupied by those more severely afflicted: delusionals such as Russell and prot, manic and deep depressives, obdurate misanthropes, and others unable to function in society. Ward Three is divided into 3A, which houses a variety of seriously psychotic individuals, and 3B, the autistic/catatonic section. Finally, Ward Four is reserved for psychopathic patients who might cause harm to the staff and their fellow inmates. This includes certain autists who regularly erupt into uncontrollable rages, as well as otherwise normal individuals who sometimes become violent without warning. The fourth floor also houses the clinic and laboratory, a small research library, and a surgical theater.

Wards One and Two are not restricted in most cases, and the patients are free to mingle. In practice, this takes place primarily in the exercise/recreation and dining rooms (Wards Three and Four maintain separate facilities). Within each ward, of course, there are segregated sleeping and bathing areas for men and women. The staff, incidentally, maintains offices and examining rooms on the fifth floor; it is a common joke among the patients that we are the craziest inmates of all.

Finally, the kitchens are spread over several floors, the laundry, heating, air-conditioning, and maintenance facilities are located in the basement, and there is an amphitheater on (and between) the first and second floors, for classes and seminars.

Before becoming acting director of the hospital I usually spent an hour or two each week in the wards just talking with my patients, on an informal basis, to get a sense of their rate of progress, if any. Unfortunately, the press of administrative duties put an end to that custom, but I still try to have lunch with them occasionally and hang around until my first interview or committee meeting or afternoon lecture. On the day after the Memorial Day weekend I decided to eat in Ward Three before looking over my notes for my three o'clock class.

Besides the autists and catatonics, this ward is populated by patients with certain disorders which would make it difficult for them to interact with those in Wards One and Two. For example, there are several compulsive eaters, who will devour anything they can get their hands on—rocks, paper, weeds, silverware; a coprophagic whose only desire is to consume his own, and sometimes others', feces; and a number of patients with severe sexual problems.

One of the latter, dubbed "Whacky" by a comedic student some time ago, is a man who diddles with himself almost constantly. Virtually anything sets him off: arms, legs, beds, bathrooms—you name it.

Whacky is the son of a prominent New York attorney and his ex-wife, a well-known television soap opera actress. As far as we know he enjoyed a fairly normal childhood, i.e., he wasn't sexually repressed or abused in any way, he owned a Lionel train and Lincoln logs, played baseball and basketball, liked to read, he had friends. In high school he was shy around girls, but in college he became engaged to a beautiful coed. Although convivial and outgoing, she was nevertheless extremely coquettish, leading him on and on but never quite going "all the way." Crazed with desire, Whacky remained as virginal as Russell for two agonizing years—he was saving himself for the woman he loved.

But on their wedding day she ran off with an old boyfriend, recently released from the state prison, leaving Whacky literally standing at the altar (and bursting at the seams). When he received the news that his fiancée had jilted him, he took down his pants and began to masturbate right there in the church, and he has been at it ever since.

Prostitution therapy was completely ineffective in Whacky's case. However, drug treatments have proven marginally successful, and he can usually come to the table and get back to his room without causing a disturbance.

When he is not caught up in his compulsion, Whacky is a very pleasant guy. Now in his mid-forties, he is still youthfully handsome, with closely cropped brown hair, a strong cleft chin, and a terrible melancholy that shows in his sad blue eyes. He enjoys watching televised sporting events and talks about the baseball or football standings whenever I see him. On this particular occasion, however, he did not discuss the Mets, his favorite team. Instead, he brought up the subject of prot.

Whacky had never seen my new patient as far as I knew, since inhabitants of Ward Three are not permitted to visit the other floors. But somehow he had heard about a visitor in Ward Two who had come from a faraway place where life was very different from ours, and he wanted to meet him. I tried to discourage the idea by downplaying prot's imaginary travels, but his pathetic baby-blue eyes were so insistent that I told him I would give the matter some thought. "But why do you want to meet him?" I inquired.

"Why, to see if he will take me back with him, of course!"

The sudden silence was eerie—the place is usually one of noisy confusion and flying food. I glanced around. No one was wailing or giggling or spitting. Everyone was watching us and listening. I mumbled something about "seeing what I could do." By the time I got up to leave, the whole of Ward Three had made it clear that they wanted a chance to take their cases to my "alien" patient, and it took me nearly half an hour to calm everyone down and make my exit.

TALKING with Whacky always reminds me of the awesome power that sex has over all of us, as Freud perceived in a moment of tremendous inspiration a century ago. Indeed, most of us have sexual problems at some time in, if not throughout, our lives.

It wasn't until my wife and I had been married for several years that it suddenly occurred to me what my father had been doing on the night he died. The realization was so intense that I leaped out of bed and stared at myself in the closet-door mirror. What I saw was my father looking back at me: same tired eyes, same graying temples, same knobby knees. It was then that I understood with crystal clarity that I was a mortal human being.

My wife was wonderfully understanding throughout the ensuing ordeal—she is a psychiatric nurse herself—though she finally insisted I seek professional help for my frustrating impotence. The only thing that came from this was the "revelation" that I harbored tremendous guilt feelings about my father's death. But it wasn't until after I finally passed the age he was when he died that the (midlife) crisis mercifully ended and I was able to resume my conjugal duties. During that miserable six-month period I think I hated my father more than ever. Not only had he chosen my career for me and precipitated a lifelong guilt complex, but, thirty years after his death, he had nearly managed to ruin my sex life as well!

S T E V E did even better than he promised. He faxed the astronomical data, including a computerized printout of a star chart of the night sky as seen from the hypothetical planet K-PAX, directly to my office. Mrs. Trexler was quite amused by the latter, referring to it as my "connect-the-dots."

Armed with this information, which prot could not possibly have had in his possession, I met with him again at the usual time on Wednesday. Of course I knew he could not be a space traveler any more than our resident Jesus Christ could have stepped out of the New Testament. But I was nonetheless curious as to just what this man could pull from the recesses of his unpredictable, though certainly human, mind.

He came into my examining room preceded by his standard Cheshire-cat grin. I was ready for him with a whole basket of fruit, which he dug into with relish. As he devoured three bananas, two oranges, and an apple he asked me a few questions about Ernie and Howie. Most patients express some curiosity about their fellow inmates and, without divulging anything confidential, I did not hesitate to answer them. When I thought he was relaxed and ready I turned on the recorder and we began.

To summarize, he knew everything about the newly discovered star system. There was some discrepancy in his description of the way K-PAX revolved around the two stars it was associated with—he claimed it was not a figure eight but something more complex—and the corresponding length of the putative planet's year was not what Steve or, rather, Dr. Flynn had calculated. But the rest of it fit quite well: the size and brightness of Agape and Satori (his K-MON and K-RIL), the periodicity of their rotation about each other, the next closest star, etc. Of course it could have been a series of lucky guesses, or perhaps he was reading my mind, though the tests showed no special aptitude for this ability. It seemed to me more likely, however, that this patient could somehow divine arcane astronomical data much like the savants mentioned earlier can make computer-like calculations and pull huge numbers from their heads. But it would have been an astonishing feat indeed if he could have constructed a picture of the night sky as seen from the planet K-PAX, which, incidentally, Professor Flynn had now chosen to call his previously unnamed planet. In anticipation of this result I think I was already contemplating the book the reader is now holding. So it was with some excitement that I nervously watched as he sketched his chart, insisting all the while that he wasn't very good at freehand drawing. I cautioned him to remember that the night sky as observed from K-PAX would look quite different from the way it does on Earth.

"Tell me about it," he replied.

It took him only a few minutes. While he was sketching I mentioned that an astronomer I knew had informed me that light travel was theoretically impossible. He stopped what he was doing and smiled at me tolerantly. "Have you ever studied your EARTH history?" he asked. "Can you think of a single new idea which all the experts in the field did not label 'impossible'?"

He returned to his diagram. As he drew he seemed to focus on the ceiling, but perhaps his eyes were closed. In any case he paid no attention to the map he was working on. It was as if he were simply copying it from an internal picture or screen. This was the result:

There are several notable features about his sketch: a "constellation" shaped like an *N* (upper right), another like a question mark (lower left), a "smiling mouth" (lower right), and an enormous eye-shaped cluster of stars (upper left). Note that he also indicated the location of the invisible Earth on his chart (center). The reason for the relatively few background stars in the diagram was, according to prot, that it never got completely dark on K-PAX, so there are fewer stars visible in the sky than one can ordinarily see, in rural areas, from the nighttime Earth.

However, it was clear that prot's and Steve's charts were completely different. Although not surprised to find that my "savant" had his limits I was, nonetheless, somewhat disappointed. I am aware that this is not a very scientific attitude, and I can only attribute it to the post-midlife-crisis syndrome first described by E. L. Brown in 1959, something that occurs most often in men who have entered their fifties: a curious desire for something interesting to happen to them.

Be that as it may, at least I would now be able to confront the patient with this contradictory evidence, which would, I hoped, help to convince him of his Earthly origin. But that would have to wait until the next session. Our time was up, and Mrs. Trexler was impatiently flashing me a telephone signal to remind me of a safety committee meeting.

ACCORDING to my notes the place was a zoo the rest of the afternoon with meetings, a problem with several of the photocopy machines, Mrs. Trexler at the dentist, and a seminar by one of the candidates for the position of permanent director. But I did find time to fax prot's star map to Steve before escorting the applicant to dinner.

The candidate, whom I shall call Dr. Choate, exhibited a rather peculiar mannerism: He continually checked his fly, presumably to make sure it was closed. Quite unconsciously, it appeared, since he did it in the conference room, in the dining room, in the wards, with women present or not. And his specialty was human sexuality! It has been said that all psychiatrists are a little crazy. Dr. Choate did nothing to dispel that canard.

I took the candidate to Asti, a lower Manhattan restaurant where the proprietor and his waiters are apt to break into an aria at the drop of a fork and encourage their patrons to do likewise. But Choate had no interest in music and finished his meal in rather glum silence. I had a lovely time, however, catching a flying doughball in my teeth and singing the part of Nadir in the lovely duet from *The Pearl Fishers*, and still made the 9:10 to Connecticut. When I got home, my wife told me Steve had called. I rang him back immediately.

"Pretty amazin' stuff!" he exclaimed.

"Why?" I said. "His drawing didn't look a thing like yours."

"Yes, Ah know. Ah thought your man had just concocted somethin' out of his head, at first. Then Ah saw where he had put in the arrow indicatin' the position of the Earth."

"So?"

"The chart Ah gave you was for the sky as seen *from* Earth, except that it was transposed seven thousand light-years away to the planet he calls K-PAX. Do you see what Ah'm sayin'? Lookin' back *here* from *there,* the sky would appear entirely different. So I went back to my computer, and *voilà!* There was the *N* constellation, the question mark, the smile, the eyeball cluster—all where he said they'd be. This *is* a joke, idn' it? Ah *know* Charlie put you up to this!"

That night I had a dream. I was floating around in space and utterly lost. No matter which direction I turned, the stars looked exactly the same to me. There was no familiar sun, no moon, not even a recognizable constellation. I wanted to go home but I had no idea which way it was. I was afraid, terrified that I was all alone in the universe. Suddenly I saw prot. He was motioning that I should follow him. Greatly relieved, I did so. As we proceeded he pointed out the eyeball cluster and all the rest, and at last I knew where I was.

Then I woke up and couldn't go back to sleep. I recalled an incident a few days earlier when I was running across the hospital lawn on my way to a consultation with the family of one of my patients. Prot was sitting on the grass clutching, it appeared, a batch of worms. I was late for an appointment and didn't dwell on it then. Later on I realized that I had never seen any of the patients playing with a handful of worms before, and where did he get them? I puzzled over this as I lay in bed awake, until I remembered his saying, in session two, that on K-PAX everything had evolved from wormlike creatures. Was he studying them as we might scrutinize our own cousins, the fishes, whose gills still manifest themselves for a time in the human embryo?

I hadn't yet found an opportunity to call Dr. Rappaport, our ophthalmologist, about the results of the vision test, but I did so the following morning. It is "highly unlikely," he told me, somewhat testily, I thought, that a human being would be able to detect light at a wavelength of three hundred angstroms. Such a person, he pointed out, would be able to see things only certain insects can see. Though he seemed extremely dubious, as if I were trying to make him the victim of a practical joke, he wouldn't go so far as to deny our examination results.

Once again I reflected on how remarkably complex the human brain really is. How can a sick mind like prot's possibly train itself to see UV light, and figure out how to diagram the sky from seven thousand light-years away? The latter was not completely outside the realm of possibility, but what an astonishing talent! Furthermore, if he *was* a savant, he was an *intelligent, amnesiacal, delusional* one. This was absolutely extraordinary, an entirely new phenomenon. And I suddenly realized: I've got my book!

S A V A N T syndrome is one of the most amazing and least understood pathologies in the realm of psychiatry. The affliction takes many forms. Some savants are "calendar calculators," meaning that they can tell you immediately what day of the week July 4, 2990 falls on, though they are often unable to learn to tie their shoes. Others can perform incredible arithmetical feats, such as to add long columns of numbers, mentally calculate large square roots, etc. Still others are wonderfully musically gifted and can sing or play back a song, or even the various parts of a symphony or opera, after a single first hearing.

Most savants are autistic. Some have suffered clinically

detectable brain damage, while others show no such obvious abnormality. But nearly all have IQs well below average, usually in the fifty to seventy-five range. Rarely has a savant been found to exhibit a normal or greater intelligence quotient.

I am privileged to have known one of these remarkable individuals. She was a woman in her sixties who had been diagnosed with a slow-growing brain tumor centered in the left occipital lobe. Because of this malignancy she was almost totally unable to speak, read, or write. She was further plagued by a nearly constant chorea and barely able to feed herself. As if that weren't enough, she was one of the most unattractive women I have ever seen. The staff called her, affectionately, "Catherine Deneuve," after the lovely French film star, who was very popular at that time.

But what an artist! When provided with suitable materials, her head and hands stopped shaking and she began to create, from memory, near-perfect reproductions of works by many of the greatest artists in history. Though they ordinarily took only a few hours to complete, her paintings are virtually indistinguishable from the originals. Amazingly, while she worked she even seemed to become beautiful!

Some of her work now resides in various museums and private collections all over the country. When she died, the family generously donated one of her pictures to the hospital, where it graces the wall of the faculty conference room. It is a perfect copy of van Gogh's "Sunflowers," the original of which hangs in the Metropolitan Museum of Art, and one is just as awestruck by her talent as by the genius of the master himself.

In the past, the emphasis has been on trying to "normalize" such individuals, to mold them into products more suitable to society's needs. Even "Catherine Deneuve" was encouraged to spend less time painting and more time learning to dress and feed herself. If not cultivated, however, these remarkable abilities can be lost, and attempts are now being made, at various institutions, to allow such people to develop their gifts to the fullest.

However, most savants are very difficult to communicate with. Normal discourse with "Catherine," for example, was impossible. But prot was alert, rational, able to function normally. What might we learn from such an individual? What else did he know about the stars, for example? Might there be more ways to arrive at knowledge than we are willing to consider or admit? There is, after all, a fine line between genius and insanity—consider, for example, Blake, Woolf, Schumann, Nijinsky, and, of course, van Gogh. Even Freud was plagued by severe mental problems. The poet John Dryden put it this way:

> *Great wits are sure to madness near alli'd*
> *And thin partitions do their bounds divide.*

I brought this up at the Monday morning staff meeting, where I proposed to let prot ramble on about whatever he wanted and try to determine whether there was anything of value he might have to tell us about his (our) world, as well as his own condition and identity. Unfortunately, despite the substantiating presence of "Catherine Deneuve" 's priceless painting, there was little enthusiasm for this idea. Indeed, Klaus Villers, without ever having seen the patient, pronounced him such a hopeless case that more aggressive measures should be instigated "at ze first suitable opportunity," though he's probably more conservative in his approach to his own patients than anyone else on the staff. The consensus, however, was that little was to be lost by giving my patient a few more weeks to have his say before turning him over to the pharmacologists and surgeons.

There was another facet to the case that I did not mention at that meeting: Prot's presence seemed to be having a positive effect on some of the other patients in his ward. For example, Ernie was taking his temperature less frequently, and Howie seemed a bit less frenetic. He even sat down one night and watched a New York Philharmonic concert on television, I was told. Some of the other patients were beginning to take a greater interest in their surroundings as well.

One of these was a twenty-seven-year-old woman whom I shall call Bess. Homeless and emaciated when she was brought to the hospital, she had never—not even once—smiled, as far as I am aware. From the time she was a child, Bess had been treated like a slave by her own family. She did all the cleaning and cooking and laundering. Her Christmas presents, when she got anything at all, consisted of utensils and appliances, a new ironing board. She felt it should have been she who perished in the fire that devastated the family's tenement apartment, rather than her brothers and sisters. It was shortly thereafter that she was brought to us, nearly frozen because she wouldn't go to one of the shelters the city provides for the homeless.

From the beginning it was difficult to get her to eat. Not, like Ernie, because she was afraid to, or like Howie, was too busy, but because she didn't think she deserved to: "Why do *I* get to eat when so many are hungry?" She was certain it was raining on the sunniest days. Everything that happened seemed to remind her of some tragedy, some terrible incident from her past. Neither electroconvulsive therapy nor a variety of neuroleptic drugs had proven effective. She was the saddest person I had ever met.

But on one of my decreasingly frequent travels through the wards I noticed that she was sitting with her knees up and her arms wrapped around them, paying rapt attention to whatever prot might choose to say. Not smiling, but not crying, either.

And seventy-year-old Mrs. Archer, ex-wife of one of America's foremost industrialists, ceased her constant muttering whenever prot was around.

Known in Ward Two as "the Duchess," Mrs. Archer takes her meals on fine china in the privacy of her own room. Trained since birth for a life of luxury, she complains constantly about the service she receives, and about everyone's deportment in general. Amazingly, the Duchess, who once ran naked for a mile down Fifth Avenue when her husband left her for a much younger woman, became a lamb in the presence of my new patient.

The only person who seemed to resent prot's proximity was Russell, who decided that prot was scouting the Earth for the devil. "Get thee behind me, Satan!" he exclaimed periodically, to no one in particular. Although many of the patients continued to flock to him for sympathy and advice, his coterie was shrinking almost daily and gravitating toward prot instead.

But the point I was making was that prot's presence seemed to be beneficial for many of our long-term patients. This raised an interesting dilemma: If we were successful in diagnosing and treating prot's illness, might not his recovery come at the expense of many of his fellow sufferers?

Session Five

B E F O R E my next encounter with prot I had a couple of old floor lamps brought in from the storage tunnel and equipped them with fifteen-watt "nightlight" bulbs, hoping the dimmer radiance would induce him to remove his dark glasses so I could see his eyes. That is exactly what happened and, although now it was too dark in my examining room to see the rest of him with clarity, I could discern his obsidian irises shining across the desk like those of some nocturnal animal as he plucked a papaya from the fruit basket and offered me a bite.

While he ate I casually gave him the date of my birth and asked him to tell me what day of the week it fell on. He shrugged and went on chomping. I asked him to give me the square root of 98,596. His reply was: "Mathematics is not my strong suit." Then I asked him to do what I thought he had done earlier, namely to draw the night sky as seen from K-PAX, only in the other direction, away from the Earth.

When he had finished I compared it with the one Steve had faxed me the week before. It contained fewer stars than the computer projection, but I could tell that the general pattern was the same.

I didn't waste time asking him how he knew what the night sky looked like from K-PAX. He would undoubtedly have snorted something about "growing up there." Instead, I turned on the tape recorder and essentially just let him ramble. I wanted to know exactly how well developed his peculiar delusion was and what, if anything, we might be able to learn from it, both about prot's true background and, perhaps, about the universe in general.

"Tell me about K-PAX," I said.

He lit up when I asked him that. Munching a star fruit, the significance of which was not lost on him, he said, "What would you like to know?"

"Everything. Describe a typical day in a typical year."

"Ah," he nodded. "A typical day." Apparently this was not an unpleasant prospect. He finished his snack, and in the dim light I could see his fingertips coming together and his eyes rolling up. It took a few seconds for him to gather his thoughts, or project them onto his internal screen, or whatever he did with them. "Well, to begin with, we don't have 'days' in the sense you mean them. We experience rather dusky light conditions most of the time, you see, much like it is in this room right now." The last phrase was accompanied by a very familiar wry grin. "Also, K-PAXians don't sleep as much as y'all do, nor do we sleep at regular times, but only as the need arises." I had gotten staff reports to this effect on prot's sleeping habits. He stayed up most of the night reading or writing or, apparently, just thinking, and napped at odd times during the day. "And finally, K-PAX doesn't rotate unidirectionally as does EARTH, but reverses itself as it reaches the end of its cycle every twenty-one of your years. Thus, the length of a 'day' varies from about one of your weeks to several months as K-PAX slows and reverses its spin."

At this point I noted down something I had forgotten to mention to Steve: Prot's description of the path of K-PAX around, or between, its suns didn't seem to match Dr. Flynn's "figure eight" pattern.

"Incidentally," he said, and his eyes opened for a moment, "we do have calendars and clocks, though we rarely use them. On the other hand, they never need to be reset or replaced—they are the type you would call 'perpetual.' But to get back to your question, let's say I have just awakened from a little snooze. What would I do? If I were hungry I would eat something. Some soaked grains, perhaps, and some fruit."

I asked him what he meant by a "soaked" grain, and to describe some K-PAXian fruits.

His eyes popped open again and he sat up straighter; he seemed to relish the opportunity to explain the details of his "world." "A soaked grain is just what it sounds like," he said. "You soak a grain long enough and it gets soft, like your rice or oatmeal. On EARTH you prefer to cook them. We just let them soak, usually in fruit juices. There are twenty-one commonly eaten grains on our PLANET, but, like yours, none is a complete food in itself. They have to be mixed to get the proper amino acid balance. My favorite combination is drak and thon and adro. It has a nutty flavor much like your cashew."

"Gesundheit."

Prot had either a well-developed sense of humor or none at all—I was never able to tell. "Thank you," he said, without blinking an eye. "Now the fruits are a different story. We have several wonderful kinds—I especially like the ones we call yorts, or sugar plums—but they can't compare with EARTH's variety, which is due primarily to your great variations in climate. To summarize: If we get hungry we grab some soaked grains, usually in fruit juice, and sit down against a balnok tree and fall to."

"What about vegetables?"

"What about them?"

"Do you have them?"

"Oh, of course. After the next snooze we might munch a bunch of krees or likas."

"Meat? Fish? Seafood?"

"No meat. No fish. No seafood. No *sea*."

"No animals of any kind?"

He tapped his glasses on the arm of his chair. "Now, gene, I've already told you about the aps and mots—remember?"

"What about pigs and cows and sheep?"

With a deep sigh: "As I pointed out in session two, we don't have any 'domesticated' beings on K-PAX. But we have *wild* pigs, *wild* cows, *wild* sheep—"

"Wild cows??"

"Well, they're called rulis, but they're much like your cows—big, cumbersome, placid. Have you ever noticed how gentle your large beings are? Your elephants and giraffes and whales, even when they are mistreated?"

"So basically you just eat and sleep on your planet?"

"Perhaps I should back up a step. When I told you that we snooze when we feel the need, you probably imagined a bed in a bedroom in a house much like the one you live in. Wroooong! It's different on K-PAX. You see, our weather is very dependable. Every day is about the same as the one before. It is usually quite warm, and it never rains. There are structures scattered around for storage of utensils and the like, for the use of anyone who happens to pass by. Food is kept there, as well as mats and musical instruments—a variety of things—but no beds. For the most part—"

"Who owns these structures?"

"No one 'owns' anything on K-PAX."

"Go on."

"For the most part we sleep out of doors—except there are no doors—usually for an hour or two, your hour, at a time. Where we won't get stepped on by an ap, of course. By the way," he interrupted himself, sitting up again, "since sexual contact is not a desirable thing on our PLANET, or on most others, men and women are free to share everything without fear or the need for guile. You might find yourself lying down for a nap near someone of the opposite gender, but you don't need to worry about what your wife or husband—or whatever—might think if he or she hears about it, or suffer embarrassment or discomfort of any kind, even though we usually wear little or no clothing. Sexual apparati are simply no big deal on K-PAX, especially since there are only two varieties and, as you know, when you've seen both, you've seen them all."

He leaned back and closed his eyes again, obviously enjoying the exposition. "Okay, we've awakened, we've eaten something, we've urinated, picked our teeth, what do we do now? Well, whatever needs to be done. Soak some more grains for next time, wipe out our bowls, fix anything that's broken. Otherwise, anything we want! Some prefer to search the skies, others observe the leafing of the trees or the antics of the aps or the behavior of the korms or homs, or play music or paint or sculpt. When I'm not traveling I usually spend most of my time in one of the libraries, which are usually filled with beings at any given time of cycle."

"Tell me more about the libraries."

"There are some books there, of course, but those are

very old, and there is something much better. Let me see if I can describe it for you." Prot's eyes rolled up again, and his fingers began tapping together, more rapidly this time. "Imagine a computer with a monitor that projects three-dimensional images complete with all-sense capability. Now suppose you are interested in ballooning. Let's say you want to know what it was like to pilot a balloon a hundred million cycles ago, before we learned how to travel with light. You just set up the computer, tap in the instructions, and there you are! You would find yourself in an ancient gondola, floating at whatever location and altitude you specified, at the authentic wind speed and direction on the date you selected. Feel the ropes in your hands and the suns on your face! Smell the trees below! Hear the korms of that time who perch on top of the bladder or join you in the gondola! Taste the fruit and nuts provided for the trip! The surface features you see below you are perfectly accurate. It is exactly like being there!" By now prot was virtually quivering with excitement.

"What happens if you fall off?"

His bright eyes opened once more and his fingers became still. "That's a question only a human being would ask! But the answer is: nothing. You would find yourself back in the library, ready for another adventure."

"What other kinds of adventures might you have?"

"Use your imagination, doc. Anything that has happened on K-PAX in the last few million years is yours to experience, in three dimensions and all senses. You could re-create your own birth, if you wanted to. Or relive any part of your life. Or that of any other being."

"These holograms—do you have any for other planets? Will you be taking something back from Earth?"

"Planetary travel is still somewhat new to us. We've

only been at it for a few hundreds of thousands of your years, mostly just scouting expeditions, and our library is rather incomplete on that subject. As for EARTH—well, I find it to be a very interesting place, and I will so state in my report. But whether anyone will want to set up all the parameters . . ." He shrugged and reached for a mango, bit into it without peeling off the skin. "But that's only the beginning!" he exclaimed, with a noisy slurp. "Suppose you are interested in geology. Tap in the instructions, and samples of any and every rock, ore, gem, slag, or meteorite, complete with name, origin, composition, chemistry, density, from whatever source you specify, will be at your fingertips. You can pick them up, feel them, smell them. Same with flora and fauna or any group or species thereof. Science. Medicine. History. The arts. You like opera, *nicht wahr?* In a matter of seconds you could select anything you wished to see and hear, from a list of everything ever written or performed on K-PAX or certain other PLANETS, organized by title, subject, setting, types of voices, composer, performers, et cetera, et cetera, all cross-referenced. If you had this capability on EARTH you could take part in a performance yourself alongside Ponselle or Caruso! Sound good?" I had to admit that it did. "Or you could sail with Columbus, sign the Magna Carta, drive the Indy Five Hundred, pitch to Babe Ruth—you name it.

"After a time in the library," he continued, a little more placidly now, "I might go for a walk in the woods or just sit or lie down somewhere for a while. That's one of the nicest things of all." He paused for a moment, apparently deep in thought, then said: "A few months ago I sat beside a pond in alabama. There was no wind at all and it was absolutely quiet, wonderfully still except for the occasional jumping of a fish or croaking of a frog or the sound of water bugs making tiny ripples on the surface. Have you ever experienced that? It is beautiful. There are no ponds on K-PAX, but the feeling is the same."

"When was this?"

"Last october." He leaned back with that perpetual smile on his face as if he were, at that moment, actually sitting beside the pond he had just described. Then he sat up and sang, rather loudly and not on key, "And that's a typical daaayyyy" (tap, tap), "in dogpatch (tap), u.s.aaayyyy." A reference, according to my son Fred, to a popular Broadway musical of the fifties called *Li'l Abner*.

And then he said something totally unexpected, something precipitated, apparently, by his "reminiscing" about life on his "world." He said, "No offense intended, gene, but my time is almost up here and I can't wait to get back."

This took me completely by surprise. I said, "What—to K-PAX?"

"Where else?"

Now it was my turn to sit up straighter. "When are you planning to return?"

Without a moment's hesitation: "On august seventeenth."

"August seventeenth. Why August seventeenth?"

He said, "It's 'Beam me up, scotty' time."

"You're 'beaming' back to K-PAX on that date?"

"Yes," he replied. "And I shall miss you. And all the other patients. And," he nodded toward the nearly empty basket, "all your delicious fruits."

I said, "Why does it have to be August seventeenth?"

"Safety reasons."

"Safety reasons?"

"You see, I can go anywhere on EARTH without fear of bumping into anyone traveling at superlight speed. But

68

beings are going to and coming from K-PAX all the time. It has to be coordinated, like your airport control towers."

"August seventeenth."

"At 3:31 A.M. Eastern time."

I was disappointed to find that our own time was up for this session. "I'd like to take this up again next week, if that's all right with you. Oh, and could you draw up a K-PAXian calendar for me some time? Just a typical cycle or so would be fine."

"Anything you say. Until august seventeenth I'm all yours. Except for a little side trip up north, of course. I haven't been to a few places yet, remember?" He was already out the door. *"Ciao,"* he called on his way down the corridor.

AFTER he had gone I returned to my office to recopy my notes. As I was trying to make some sense of them I found myself gazing at Chip's picture sitting on my desk. *"Ciao"* is one of his favorite expressions, along with "Truly," and "You know?" Now on summer vacation, he had gotten a job as a lifeguard at one of the public beaches. A good thing, too, since he had already weaseled two years' advances on his allowance. The last of my children, soon out of the nest.

I should wax philosophical here and report that I pondered long and hard the implications of that inevitable fledging, both for Chip and for myself, but the truth is that it brought me back to prot's "departure date." August seventeenth was only two months away. What did it mean? It would be like Russell's saying that on such-and-such a day he would be returning to heaven. But in all the years he had been with us Russell has never announced a date for that journey and, to my knowledge, neither has any other delusional. It was totally unprecedented in the annals of psychiatry. And since it was patently impossible for prot to travel to K-PAX, or anywhere else, what would happen to him on that day? Would he withdraw completely into his amnesiacal armor? The only possible way I could see to prevent that from happening would be to find out who this man really was and where he had come from before it was too late.

But suddenly it occurred to me that August seventeenth would have been the approximate date that prot claimed he had arrived on Earth nearly five years earlier. With this in mind I asked Mrs. Trexler to put in a call to the precinct where he had been brought in originally, as indicated on his admission records, to request that they check whether anyone answering his description had disappeared on or about that particular date. And to inform them of prot's possible visit to Alabama in October. She came in later with a batch of letters for me to sign, and mentioned that the police had promised to let us know if anything turned up. "But don't hold your breath," she snorted.

W E find out a lot about our patients not only from the nursing staff but also from the other inmates, who love to talk about one another. Thus it was from his roommate Ernie that I first learned that Howie had become an entirely different person—cheerful, even relaxed! I went to see for myself.

Ernie was right. On a cool Thursday afternoon I found him calmly sitting in the wide sill of the second-floor lounge gazing out the window toward the sky. No dictionaries, no encyclopedias, no counting the threads in the big green carpet. His glasses, whose lenses were usually fogged with grime, had been cleaned.

I requested permission to sit down with him, and struck up a casual conversation pertaining to the flowers lining the high wall on the other side of the lawn. He was happy to produce, as he had many times in the past, the common and Latin names of each of them, something of their genetic history, nutritional value, medical and industrial uses. But he never took his eyes from the dark gray sky. He seemed to be looking for something—*scanning* was the word that came to mind. I asked him what it was.

"The bluebird," he said.

"The bluebird?"

"The bluebird of happiness."

That was an odd thing for Howie to say. He might well have known everything about bluebirds, from their eye color to their migratory habits to the total number worldwide. But *the* bluebird? Of *happiness?* And where did he get that gleam in his eye? When I pressed him on this I learned that he had gotten the idea from prot. Indeed, my problem patient had assigned Howie this "task," the first of three. I didn't know at the time what the other two were, and neither did Howie. But the first was assigned and accepted: Find the bluebird of happiness.

Some of the temporaries in Ward One quickly dubbed Howie "the bluenerd of sappiness," and in Ward Four there was talk of a bluebeard stalking the grounds, but Howie was oblivious to all this. Indeed, he was as single-minded as ever toward his illusive goal. Nevertheless, I was struck by the placidity with which he had taken up his stint by the window. Gone were the fitful checking and rechecking, the rushing from book to book, the feverish scratching of pen on reams and reams of paper. In fact, his tablets and ledgers were still spread out all over his desk and the little table he shared with Ernie; apparently he had dropped what he was doing and didn't even care enough about his lifetime of records and notes to file them away. It was such a refreshing sight to see him calmly sitting at the window that I could not help but breathe a sigh of relief myself, as if the weight of the world had been lifted from my own shoulders, as well as Howie's.

Just before I left him the sun came out, illuminating the flowers and bathing the lawn in gold. Howie smiled. "I never noticed how beautiful that is," he said.

Thinking that hell would freeze over before he spotted a bluebird in upper Manhattan I didn't bother to change his semiannual interview, scheduled for September, to an earlier date. But it was only a few days later, on a warm, drizzly morning that the wards were filled with the rare and delightful sound of a happy voice crying, "Bluebird! Bluebird!" Howie was running down the corridors (I didn't witness this personally, but Betty told me about it later), bursting into the exercise room and the quiet room, interrupting card games and meditation, finally grabbing a smiling prot by the hand and tugging him back to the lounge, shouting, "Bluebird! Bluebird!" By this time, of course, all the patients—and staff, too—were rushing to see the bluebird for themselves, and the windows were full of faces peering out at the wet lawn, shouting "Bluebird!" as they spotted it, until everyone was shouting "Bluebird! Bluebird! Bluebird!" Ernie and Russell and even the Duchess were caught up in the excitement. Betty said she could almost hear movie music playing. Only Bess seemed unmoved by the event, recalling all the dead and injured birds she had encountered in her joyless lifetime.

Eventually the bluebird flew away and everything settled back to normal, or almost so. Or was there a subtle change? A gossamer thread of something—hope, maybe?—had been left by the bird, and someone rushed out to retrieve it. It was so fine that, after it had dried out, no one could actually see it, except for prot, perhaps. It remains in Ward Two today, passed invisibly from patient to patient as a sort of talisman to alleviate depression and replace it with hope and good cheer. And, amazingly, it often works.

Session Six

M y next session with prot took place the following afternoon. Smiling profusely when he came into my examining room, he handed me what he called a "calendar." It was in the form of a scroll, and so complicated that I could make little sense of it. But I thanked him and motioned to the basket of fruit on the side table by his chair.

I waited to see if he would bring up the subject of Howie and the bluebird, but he never mentioned it. When I finally asked him about it he bit into a cantaloupe and shrugged. "It had been there all the time, but nobody had looked for it." I didn't mention the larger issue of his assigning "tasks" to the patients. As long as the results were positive, I decided to allow it for the time being.

After he had finished the last kiwi, fuzz and all, I turned on the tape recorder. "I'd like to follow up on something you told me earlier."

"Why not?"

"I believe you said there is no government on K-PAX, and no one works. Is that right?"

"Quoit roit, guvnuh."

"I must be dense. I still don't understand how things get done. Who builds the libraries and makes all the equipment for them and installs it and runs it? Who makes all the holographic software, if that's the proper terminology? Who makes your eating utensils and your clothes? Who plants the grains? What about all the other things that you surely need and use on K-PAX?"

Prot smacked his forehead with the palm of his hand and muttered, *"Mama mia."* Then, "All right. Let me see if I can make it simple enough for you to understand." He leaned forward in his chair and fixed me with his penetrating black gaze, as he did whenever he wanted to make sure I was paying attention. "In the first place, we hardly ever wear any clothing on K-PAX. Except once each cycle—every twenty-one of your years—when we have some cold weather. And nobody plants the grains. You leave them alone and they plant themselves. As for the libraries, if something needs to be done, someone does it, *capisci?* This goes for everything you would call 'goods and services.' What could be simpler?"

"Surely there are jobs no one wants to do. Hard labor, for example, or cleaning public toilets. That's only human nature."

"There are no humans on K-PAX."

I glared back at him. "Oh yes, I forgot."

"Besides, there is nothing that needs to be done that is really unpleasant. Look. You defecate, don't you?"

"Not as often as I'd like."

"Do you find it unpleasant?"

"Somewhat."

"Do you get someone to do it for you?"

"I would if I could."

"But you don't, and you don't think twice about it. You just do it. And it does have its rewards, right?"

The tape indicates that I chuckled here. "Okay. There are no undesirable jobs. But what about the other side of the coin? What about the specialty jobs that take a lot of training? Like medicine. Or law. Who does those?"

"We have no laws, therefore no lawyers. As for the former, everyone practices medicine, so, in general, there is no need for doctors, either. Of course there are some who are more interested in such matters than are others, and they are available whenever anybody needs them. For surgery, primarily."

"Tell me more about medicine on your planet."

"I knew you'd get around to that sooner or later." He settled back into his familiar pose. "As I suggested a moment ago, there isn't much need for it on K-PAX. Since we eat only plants, we have almost no circulatory problems. And since there's no pollution of our air or our food, and no tobacco, there isn't much cancer, either. There's little stress, ergo no GI problems. Also there are few serious accidents, no suicide, no crime—*voilà!* Not much need for doctors! But of course there are occasional outbreaks of disease. Most of these run their course without permanent damage, but there are a few serious afflictions. For these we again have the plants. There is an herb or two for every ailment. You just have to look it up in the library."

"You have an herb for *everything*?"

"So do you. For aids, for all the different kinds of cancer, for parkinson's and alzheimer's, for blocked arteries. Herbs for selective anesthesia. They're all there, in your tropical forests. All you have to do is look for them."

"Selective anesthesia?"

"If you want to do abdominal surgery, there is something to anesthetize that part of the body. You can watch someone take out your appendix. Or do it yourself, if you wish. And so on. Your chinese have the right idea with their acupuncture."

"Are there hospitals?"

"More like small clinics. One for each village."

"What about psychiatry? I suppose you're going to tell me there's no need for it on K-PAX."

"Why should there be? We don't have religious or sexual or financial problems to tear us apart."

"All right. But aren't there those who become mentally ill for organic reasons? What do you do with *them*?"

"Again, these are rare on our PLANET. But such beings are usually not dangerous and are not locked up for the convenience of others. On the contrary, they are well taken care of by everyone else."

"You mean your mental patients aren't treated with any drugs—herbs—to make them well?"

"Mental illness is often in the eye of the beholder. Too often on this PLANET it refers to those who think and act differently from the majority."

"But surely there are those who are obviously unable to cope with reality. . . ."

"Reality is what you make it."

"So no K-PAXians are ever treated for mental problems?"

"Only if they are unhappy, or request it themselves."

"And how do you know whether they are happy or not?"

"If you don't know that, you can't be much of a psychiatrist."

"All right. You said there are no countries and no governments on K-PAX. I deduce from this that there are no armies or military weapons anywhere on your world—is that right?"

"Heaven forbid."

"Tell me—what happens if K-PAX is attacked by inhabitants of another planet?"

"A contradiction in terms. Any beings who would destroy another WORLD always destroy themselves first."

"Then what about your internal affairs? Who keeps order?"

"K-PAX is already orderly."

"But you also said there are no laws on your planet. Correct?"

"Kee-reck."

"Without laws, how does one know what is right and what is wrong?"

"The same way human beings do. Your children don't study law, do they? When they make mistakes, these are pointed out to them."

"Who decides what a 'mistake' is?"

"Everyone knows."

"How? Who created the original behavior codes?"

"No one. They just became obvious over a period of time."

"Would you say there is some moral basis for these codes?"

"Depends on your definition of 'moral.' I presume you are thinking about religion."

"Yes."

"As I said before, we have no religions on K-PAX, thank god."

"God?"

"That was a joke." Prot entered something into his notebook. "Have you no sense of humor on this PLANET?"

"Then you don't believe in God?"

"The idea was kicked around for a few hundred cycles, but it was soon rejected."

"Why?"

"Why kid ourselves?"

"But if it gives comfort . . ."

"A false hope gives only false comfort."

"Do all K-PAXians share this view?"

"I imagine. It's not something that's discussed very much."

"Why not?"

"How often do you discuss dragons and unicorns?"

"What sorts of things *are* discussed on your planet?"

"Information. Ideas."

"What sorts of ideas?"

"Can one travel forward in time? Is there a fourth spatial dimension? Are there other UNIVERSES? Stuff like that."

"One more thing before we move on to something else. What happens—I know this is rare—but what happens when someone breaks one of your behavior codes? Refuses to conform?"

"Nothing."

"Nothing?"

"We reason with him or her."

"That's all?"

"Yes."

"What if he kills someone?"

Somewhat agitated: "Why would any being do a thing like that?"

"But what if someone did?"

"We would try to avoid him or her."

"But is there no compassion for the person he has killed? Or for his next victim?"

Prot was staring at me, disgustedly it appeared, or perhaps in disbelief. "You're making a mountain out of a molehill. Beings don't kill other beings on K-PAX. Crime is less popular than sex, even. There's simply no need for it."

I had a hunch I was on to something here. "But if someone did commit a crime, shouldn't such a person—uh, being—be locked up for the good of everyone else?"

Prot was clearly becoming irate. "Let me tell you something, doc," he almost snarled. "Most humans subscribe to the policy of 'an eye for an eye, a life for a life.' Many of your religions are famous for this formula, which is well known throughout the UNIVERSE for its stupidity. Your christ and your buddha had a different vision, but nobody paid any attention to them, not even the christians and buddhists. On K-PAX there is no crime, you dig? And if there were, there would be no punishment. Apparently this is impossible for EARTH beings to understand, but it's the secret of life, believe me!" By now prot's eyes were bugging and his breathing was hard. I sensed it was time to end the day's session, if somewhat prematurely.

"I admit you have a point there. And by the way, I'm afraid I'm going to have to cut our session a little short today. I hope you don't mind. I have an important meeting which couldn't be rescheduled. Would it be all right with you if we continue with this next week?"

Calmer now, but not much: "Perfectly." Without another word he got up and stalked out.

I sat in my examining room for a few minutes after he had gone, thinking. Until that moment I had seen no evidence of anger, and rarely even a frown, in this patient. Now it appeared that just below the surface lay a seething cauldron, a volcano that could erupt at any time. Had it erupted in the past? Hysterical amnesia sometimes results from a violent and irreversible act. Had prot, in fact, killed someone, possibly on August 17, 1985? As a precaution, should I have him transferred to Ward Four?

I decided against the latter move, which might have driven him deeper into his seemingly impenetrable shell. Besides, all this was pure speculation at this point. And even if correct, he was unlikely to become violent unless we made substantial progress toward unraveling his past actions, the precipitants of his amnesia, a development I welcomed. Nevertheless, I would notify the staff and security office of the potential problem, have him watched more closely, and conduct subsequent interviews with greater caution. I decided also to notify the police department about a possible violent altercation some five years earlier, hoping it would help them to track him down, something our previous clues had failed to do.

But August seventeenth was fast approaching. I was frustrated and tired. Perhaps, I thought, I was getting too old for clinical work. Maybe I wasn't good enough any more. Maybe I never was.

I never wanted to be a psychiatrist. I wanted to be a singer.

As a pre-med student in college my only real interest was the annual "Follies Brassière," a talent show for students and faculty, in which I shamelessly belted out Broadway tunes and opera arias, to loud and addictive applause. By the time I graduated, however, I was already married and it made no sense to pursue such a frivolous dream. I was no Don Quixote.

Thus, it wasn't until I got into medical school itself that

81

I began to have serious doubts about my choice of profession. But just as I was about to confess to my new wife that I might rather try something else, Mother was diagnosed with liver cancer. Although the doctors decided to operate, it turned out to be far too late.

Mother was a courageous woman, though, and she put up a good front until the end. As she was being wheeled into surgery she talked about all the places she wanted to visit and all the things she wanted to take up: watercolors, French, the piano. But she must have known the truth. Her last words to me were, "Be a good doctor, son." She passed away on the operating table, never to see her first grandchild, who was born three months later.

There was only one other moment when I almost decided to chuck the whole thing. It was the afternoon I saw my first cadaver.

He was a forty-six-year-old white male, overweight, balding and unshaven. As we started to work on him his eyes popped open, and they seemed to be appealing to me for help. It wasn't that it made me feel faint or nauseated—I had been on too many hospital rounds as a boy—it was that the body looked exactly like my father the night he died. I had to leave.

When I told Karen what had happened, that I couldn't cut into someone that looked like my own father, she said, "Don't be silly." So I went back and opened that man's arms and legs and chest and abdomen, all the time hearing my father, who considered himself something of a comedian, whispering in my ear, "Ouch, that hurts." But I was more certain than ever that I didn't want to be an internist or surgeon. Instead, I followed the example set by my friend Bill Siegel, and went into psychiatry. Not only because it seemed less sanguinary, but also because it appeared to be a great challenge—so very little seemed to be known about the subject. Unfortunately, that sad state of affairs is as true today as it was nearly thirty years ago.

THE afternoon that prot stalked out of my examining room I got a call from a freelance reporter who was planning to do a story on mental illness for a national magazine. She wanted to know whether she might be able to "set up shop" at MPI for a few weeks to gather background material and "pick our brains," as she put it. That's a phrase I've never liked much, along with "eat your heart out" and "chew someone out"—I think of vultures. However, it was hardly a basis for rejecting her proposal, and I gave her tentative approval to do the article, hoping that the notoriety might get us some additional dollars. I transferred her call to Mrs. Trexler to arrange for an appointment at a time convenient for both of us. I laughed right into the phone when she said that "now" was convenient for her.

A new patient of Dr. Goldfarb's arrived over the weekend. I'll call him "Chuck" because, although that is not his name, that is what he wanted to be called. Chuck was a sixty-three-year-old New York City doorman—or doorperson, as Abby would have it—and a chronic cynic, hopeless pessimist, and classic curmudgeon. He was brought in because he was beginning to inform everyone who walked into his building that he or she "stunk." Everyone within fifty miles of him "stunk." Indeed, his first words, when he entered the hospital, were, "This place stinks." Bald as an eightball and somewhat cross-eyed, he might have made an almost comic figure had not his presence in Ward Two brought terror to the heart of Maria—he reminded her of her father.

Maria had been at MPI for three years and, in all that

time, Russell was the only male who could get near her. At first she had numerous Sunday visitors, as befit her large family, including cousins of all ages. But the visitations soon dwindled to her mother and the odd aunt or uncle every month or two for the simple reason that when they came to see Maria they often found someone else: Maria suffered from multiple personality disorder.

MPD begins to manifest itself in early childhood as an attempt to deal with a terrible physical or mental trauma from which there appears to be no escape. Maria wasn't beaten, Natalie was; Maria wasn't molested, it was Julia; Maria can't bear these attacks but Debra is strong. Many of the victims harbor scores of distinct personalities, depending on the number and severity of the abuses, but the average is about a dozen, each of whom is able to "take over" under certain circumstances. For reasons that are unclear, instances of a single alter ego are relatively rare.

Personality differences among the various alters are often astonishing. Some are much smarter than others, express widely discrepant talents, score uniquely on psychological tests, and even produce disparate EEG patterns! They might also visualize themselves as being very dissimilar in appearance, or even of a different sex, than that of the other identities. Whether these are true individuals is questionable, but, until integration occurs, many of the alters, including the "primary" personality, may be totally unaware of what the others are doing when in control of the body.

Maria was known to harbor more than a hundred separate and distinct personalities, most of whom rarely made an appearance. Otherwise her case is typical for this disorder. She had been raped innumerable times by her father, starting when she was barely three years old. Her devoutly religious mother, who cleaned a dozen large offices at night, never knew about these violations, and her older brothers had been threatened into silence until they were old enough to demand some of the "action" for themselves. Under such circumstances life can become quite unbearable and the desire for escape overwhelming.

A pretty girl with long black hair that shines like the stars, Maria came to us after she, as Carmen, had nearly scratched a boy's eyes out when he tried to make advances. Until that incident she was thought of as "quiet" and "distant." No one has touched her since, with the possible exception of Russell, who, of course, refers to her as "Mother."

But Maria herself is seldom in evidence. Most of the time one of the others is in charge, one of her "defenders" or "protectors." Sometimes, when one of her "persecutors" takes control, we see another facet of Maria, a darker side. One of these, who calls herself Carlotta, has tried to kill Maria, and therefore herself and all the others, on at least two occasions. It is this constant struggle for control among the various identities, often accompanied by anxiety, insomnia, and ceaseless headaches, that makes for the singular horror of the multiple personality sufferer.

Chuck thought *all* of Maria's alters stunk. Also Russell, Mrs. Archer, Ernie and Howie, and even harmless little Bess. The entire staff, including myself, stunk to high heaven. To his credit he admitted that he, himself, smelled worse than all the rest of us put together—"like a gutwagon," as he put it. The only person in the entire hospital who did not stink, in his opinion, was prot.

Session Seven

BECAUSE of what had happened at the end of our previous encounter I asked Mr. Jensen and Mr. Kowalski to stand by during session seven. However, prot seemed in unusually good spirits as he chomped on a pineapple. "How was your meeting?" he said with his familiar grin.

It took me a moment to figure out what this meant, but I finally remembered the "important meeting" I had dismissed him with at the end of session six. I told him it had gone well. He seemed pleased to hear this. Or was it a smirk? In any case the clock was moving and I turned on the tape recorder. I also switched on my backup machine, this one to play back a Schubert song I had recorded earlier. When it was finished, I asked him to sing it back to me. He couldn't even hum the first phrase. Obviously music was not one of his talents. Nor was sculpture. I asked him to create a human head with a piece of clay—the result looked more like Mr.

Peanut. He couldn't even draw a house or a tree. It all came out looking like the work of a third-grader.

All of this, however, took up half our session. "Okay," I said, somewhat disappointedly, "last time we talked about medicine on K-PAX, or the lack of it. Tell me about your science in general."

"What would you like to know?"

"Who does it and how is it done? Are there, in fact, any scientists?"

"We are all scientists on K-PAX."

"I knew you were going to say that."

"Most human beings I've met have a rather negative opinion of science. They think it is dull and abstruse, possibly even dangerous. But everyone, even on EARTH, is a scientist, really, whether he realizes it or not. Anyone who has ever watched and wondered how a bird flies or a leaf unfurls, or concluded anything on the basis of his own observations, is a scientist. Science is a part of life."

"Well, are there any formal laboratories on K-PAX?"

"They are part of the libraries. Of course the whole UNIVERSE is a laboratory. Anyone can observe."

"What sorts of scientific observations do K-PAXians usually carry out?"

"Every species now living on our PLANET, or that ever lived there, or on several other PLANETS, is catalogued and thoroughly described. The same for the rocks. The same for the STARS and other ASTRONOMICAL OBJECTS. Every medicinal herb and what it can do is indexed. All this from millions and millions of years of observing and recording."

"And what goes on in the laboratories?"

"Oh, identifying the odd new compound that might turn up in a novel plant variant, for example."

"You mean its chemistry?"

"Yes."

"I assume your chemists can produce all these natural products synthetically. Why do you still get them from plants?"

"No one ever 'synthesizes' anything on K-PAX."

"Why not?"

"What's the point?"

"Well, you might find a useful new drug, for example. Or a better floor wax."

"We have a herbal preparation for every known disease. And we don't have floors to wax. Why should we make red grass or blue trees?"

"You're saying that everything is already known."

"Not everything. That's why I'm here."

"Aside from the occasional interstellar trip, though, it sounds pretty dull living on your planet."

He snapped back with: "Is it any duller than on EARTH? Whose inhabitants spend most of their lives trying to get laid, watching sitcoms on television, and grunting for money?"

I noted down this sudden outburst and remarked, casually: "I mean it seems pretty dull with nothing much left to discover."

"Gene, gene, gene." It sounded like a bell tolling. "No single *individual* knows very much. No matter how much one learns, there is always more to know."

"But *someone* already knows it."

"Have you ever listened to a mozart symphony?"

"Once or twice."

"Is it dull the second time, or the third, or the twentieth?"

"No, if anything . . ."

"Exactly."

"What about physics?"

"What about it?"

"Are all the laws of physics known?"

"Have you ever heard of heisenberg?"

"Yes, I've heard of him."

"He was wrong."

"With that in mind, what can you tell us about the fundamental laws of the universe? Light travel, for example."

His customary smile became even broader than usual. "Nothing."

"Nothing?"

"Nothing."

"Why not?"

"If I told you, you'd blow yourselves up. Or worse, someone else."

"Perhaps you could tell me one thing, at least. What do you use for power on K-PAX?"

"That I can tell you because you have it already, or soon will. We use type one and type two solar energies. Except for traveling, and certain other processes, when we use that of light. You'd be surprised how much energy there is in a beam of light."

"What are type one and type two solar energies?"

"Type one is the energy of the stars: nuclear fusion. The other is the type of radiation that warms your planet."

"Isn't there enough of the fusion type? Why do you need the other?"

"Spoken like a true homo sapiens."

"Meaning?"

"You humans just can't seem to learn from your mistakes. You finally discover that burning all that coal and oil and wood destroys your air and your climate. Then what do you do but go hell-bent after solar, wind, geothermal, and tidal energy without any thought whatsoever about the consequences. People!" He sighed and wagged his head.

"You haven't answered my question."

"Isn't it obvious? The use of one produces heat; the other consumes it. The net effect is that we neither warm nor cool our planet. And there is no waste or pollution."

"Have you always been able to tap these energy sources?"

"Of course not. Only for the last few billion years."

"What about before that?"

"Well, we fooled around with magnetic fields for a while, and bacterial decay and the like. But we soon realized that no matter what we tried, there was some effect or other on our air, or our temperature, or our climate. Gravitation energy is even worse. So we made do with our muscles until someone figured out how to fuse atoms safely."

"Who figured that out?"

"You mean his name?"

"Yes."

"I have no idea. We don't worship heroes on K-PAX."

"What about nuclear fission?"

"Impossible. Our beings rejected it immediately."

"Why? Because of the danger of an accident?"

"That is a small matter compared to the waste that's produced."

"You never found anything to contain it?"

"Where would we find something that lasts forever?"

"Let's turn to astronomy. Or better yet, cosmology."

"One of my favorite subjects."

"Tell me: What is the fate of the universe?"

"Fate?"

"Is it going to collapse back on itself, or will it go on expanding forever?"

"You'll love this: both."

"Both?"

"It will collapse, then expand again, then repeat and repeat and repeat."

"I don't know whether to take any comfort in that or not."

"Before you decide—there's more."

"More?"

He guffawed, the first time I had ever heard him laugh. "When the UNIVERSE expands again, everything will be as it was before!"

"You mean—"

"Exactly. Whatever mistakes you made this time around you will live through again on the next pass, over and over and over, forever and ever, amen!" His demeanor had suddenly changed. For a second I thought he was going to break into tears. But he quickly became himself again, smiling and confident.

"How do you know that? It's not possible to know that, is it?"

"It's not possible to test that hypothesis, no."

"Then how can you be sure your hypothesis is right? Or any of your other theories?"

"I'm here, ain't I?"

Something suddenly occurred to me. "I'm glad you brought that up. There's one thing you could do for me that would erase any doubts I might have about your story. Do you know what I'm suggesting?"

"I was wondering when that would occur to you." He scribbled something in his notebook.

"When could you give me a little demonstration?"

"How about right now?"

"That would be quite acceptable."

"Shalom," he said. "Aloha." But of course he just sat there grinning at me like a Cheshire cat.

"Well?"

"Well what?"

"When are you going?"

"I'm already back."

I'd been taken in by the old "fastest gun in the West" routine. "I was hoping you would stay away long enough that I might notice your absence."

"You will next week when I leave for canada, iceland, and greenland."

"Next week? I see. And how long will you be gone?"

"A few days." While I was jotting down the suggestion that we increase the surveillance on him, he exclaimed: "Well, I see our time is up, and gunnar and roman are waiting!"

I was still writing, but I vaguely recalled that the clock was positioned in such a way that prot couldn't possibly have seen it. And who told him that Jensen and Kowalski were standing by? I mumbled, "Shouldn't I decide that?" But when I looked up he was already gone.

I rewound the last part of the tape and switched it on. His assertion, in a thick, choked voice, that he was going to have to repeat his mistakes over and over for all time suddenly seemed very moving, and I wondered again: What in God's name had he done? Unless I could find some way to break through his amnesia armor it was going to be very difficult to find out. In the absence of some clue to his background I was literally working in the dark. Given enough time I might have been able to come up with such a lead, and I dearly wished I could increase the number of sessions to twice a week or even more, but I simply had no extra time. There just wasn't enough time.

A couple of days later, after returning from my Friday morning radio talk show where I answer general questions about mental health called in by the listening audience, I discovered that prot had assigned a second task to Howie. The assignment: to cure Ernie of his fear of death.

I could see what he was getting at with his "program" for Howie and perhaps I, as his staff doctor, should have thought of it myself: By encouraging him to focus on a single project, his attention was drawn away from the awesome multiplicity of life's possibilities. I still had mixed feelings about prot's assigning "tasks" to his fellow patients, but as long as no harm came from these endeavors, I continued to allow it.

Howie approached the problem in a typically methodical manner. After scrutinizing his roommate for hours on end, to the point that Ernie finally ran screaming from the room, he asked me for texts on human anatomy and physiology, specifically on the subject of respiration. I assumed he was going to try to prove to him how unusual it is for someone to choke to death, or perhaps construct some sort of breathing apparatus for Ernie's use in case the worst happened. I could see no reason to refuse him on this and I allowed him access to the fourth-floor library. In retrospect I should have realized that these solutions would have been too simplistic for someone as brilliant as Howie. Perhaps my judgment was clouded by the unconscious hope that he might somehow succeed where I had failed, and that both might find a little peace at long last.

Ernie, in the meantime, was doing much the same thing

for some of the other patients; that is, he was beginning to take an interest in their problems as well as his own. For example, he was reading poetry to blind old Mrs. Weathers, who cocked her snowy head with every word like a rapt chicken. He had always spent quite a bit of time with Russell, seeking solace primarily, but now he was chatting with the latter about a variety of secular matters—suggesting he get some exercise, for example.

He was spending a lot of time with prot also, as were most of his fellow patients, asking him about K-PAX and other supposedly inhabited regions of the universe. These talks seemed to raise their spirits enormously, or so I was informed by several of the nurses. I finally asked Ernie point-blank what it was about his discussions with prot that seemed to cheer him up so dramatically. His eyebrows lifted a mile high behind his surgical mask and he told me exactly what Whacky had said earlier, "I'm hoping he'll take me with him when he goes back!" I realized then what was drawing the others to our "alien" visitor: the promise of salvation. Not just in the hereafter, but in *this* life, and in the relatively near future. I made a note to talk to prot about this as soon as possible. It was one thing to make a sick person feel better. It was quite another to prop him up temporarily with false hopes, as he himself had asserted. But for the next few days I was unable to ask him anything. He had disappeared!

A search of the building and grounds was initiated immediately upon learning that prot had not shown up for lunch on Sunday, but no trace of him was found. No one had seen him leave the hospital, and none of the security tapes showed him passing through any locked doors or gates.

His room provided no clue as to where he might have gone. As always the bed was made and his desk and dresser were uncluttered. There wasn't even a scrap of paper in his wastebasket.

None of the patients would admit to having any knowledge of prot's whereabouts, yet none was particularly surprised that he was gone. When I asked Chuck about it he replied, "Don't worry—he'll be back."

"How do you know that?"

"Because he took his dark glasses with him."

"What has that got to do with it?"

"When he returns to K-PAX he won't need them."

Some days later a maintenance worker reported that some of the items in the storage tunnel had been shifted around. Whether prot had been hiding there, however, was never determined.

FOR his first twenty-seven years Russell never saw another human being except for his mother and father. His schooling consisted exclusively of Bible reading, four hours every morning and evening. There was no radio, and no one ever came up the long driveway because of the mud and the Doberman pinschers. In the afternoons he was expected to work in the garden or help with the chores. This isolated existence continued until a determined census worker, who also bred Dobermans, stumbled upon him accidentally while his father was at the hardware store and his mother in the back yard hanging out the wash. After he chased the astonished woman down the driveway shouting, "Mary Magdelene, I forgive you!" she reported the matter to the authorities.

Psychotherapy was completely ineffective in Russell's case, and Metrazole shock therapy barely less so. Nevertheless, he was returned to his parents. The young delusional soon escaped from the farm, however, only to be arrested as a "public nuisance." After that he was in and out of jails and hospitals for several years until he was finally brought to MPI, where he has remained to this day.

Neither Howie, who is Jewish, nor Mrs. Archer ("I'm Episcopalian," she would sniff) have ever had much use for Russell. But with his retinue shrinking rapidly—only Maria, and a few of her alters, seemed to be paying any attention to him—he began to preach the gospel to Howie and to the Duchess, who had begun to emerge from her room on occasion to speak with prot.

Howie simply ignored him, but it was different for Mrs. Archer. It would be a bad joke to state that he was driving her crazy, but that was the net effect. Conversing with Russell requires a certain amount of forbearance under the best of circumstances. He tends to preach right into your face, releasing prodigious amounts of spittle with almost every word. And when she was able to escape his fervent hectoring she found herself being assaulted by Chuck's observations, expressed in no uncertain terms, that she stunk.

Mrs. Archer, who used nearly a pint of expensive perfumes weekly, was both mortified and irate. "I most certainly do not stink!" she screeched, impatiently lighting a cigarette.

"Those goddamn things reek," Chuck would badger.

She was finally reduced to tears. "Please," she implored, when I happened by. "Let him come back."

"He wouldn't take a stinker like you with him. He's going to take me!" Chuck proclaimed.

But Russell warned, "For there shall arise false Christs, and false prophets, and they shall show great signs and wonders; insomuch that, if it were possible, they shall deceive the very elect!"

"You stink too!" Chuck reminded him.

* * *

96

DURING a quick lunch in the doctors' dining room Dr. Goldfarb told me more about Chuck. He had been a middle-level government employee at one time, she said, but blew the whistle on the waste and corruption in his division at the Pentagon. For his efforts he was fired and, for all practical purposes, blackballed, both from government and corporate employment. That alone might be cause enough for disillusionment, but the straw that broke his back was his wife's divorcing him after thirty-five years of marriage. "I couldn't have been happier," he muttered to Dr. Goldfarb. "I had to kiss that malodorous maw every day. P.U.! Stinkeroonie!" But the truth was that he loved his wife passionately and it was more than he could bear. Indeed, he had tried to commit suicide shortly after she left him by blowing his brains out with a shotgun. It must seem incredible to the reader to learn that he missed, but the fact is that many attempted suicides end in "failure" for the simple reason that they are actually desperate attempts to draw attention to the sufferer's terrible, and often silent, unhappiness. Most victims don't actually want to die; they want to communicate.

Of course, not all those who feel rootless or valueless resort to this futile measure. A manic-depressive once assured me that he would never try to kill himself. I asked him how he could be so sure. "Because," he told me, "I still haven't read *Moby Dick*."

As good a reason for living as any, I suppose, and perhaps it explains why so few people have ever finished that book.

IN the midst of all the furor surrounding prot's disappearance, the reporter who had called me the previous week arrived, half an hour early, for her appointment. She was older than she appeared, thirty-three, she said, though she looked more like sixteen. She wore faded jeans, an old checked shirt, and running shoes with no socks. My first impression was that freelance writing must be a poorly paid profession, but I eventually came to realize that she dressed this way for effect—to induce people to feel at ease. To that end she also wore little makeup, and only a hint of perfume that somehow brought to mind our summer place in the Adirondacks. "Pine woods," I would have called it. She was short, about five-two, and her teeth were tiny, like a little girl's. Disarmingly, she curled up into the chair I offered. She asked me to call her Giselle.

She came from a little town in northern Ohio. After graduating with a degree in journalism from the local college she came directly to New York, where she got a job on the now-defunct *Weekly Gazette*. She stayed there nearly eight years before writing an article on drugs and AIDS in Harlem, which won her the Cassady prize. I asked her about the dangers she must have faced researching that story. A friend had accompanied her, she explained, an ex-football player whom everyone in the area knew. "He was huge," she added with a coy smile.

She later quit the *Gazette* to research and write pieces on a variety of subjects—abortion, oil spills, and homelessness—for various periodicals, including several major newspapers and national magazines. She had also written scripts for a number of TV documentaries. She had gotten the idea to do something on mental illness after trying to find background material on Alzheimer's disease and failing to find a good generalized account of the subject "in layperson's language." Her credentials were certainly impressive, and I gave her the go-ahead to "cruise the corridors," as she put it, provided that she was accompanied by a staff member at all times, and that she enter the psychopathic ward for no more than three one-hour visits and only in the presence of a security officer. She cheerfully agreed to abide by these conditions. Nevertheless I asked Betty to keep an eye on her.

Session Eight

I was in a very bad mood when Wednesday afternoon came around, having spent the entire morning waiting to testify in a preliminary hearing, only to have the case resolved out of court. I was glad it was settled, but annoyed that half a day had been wasted, and I had missed lunch as well. Underlying all this, of course, was my concern about prot's well-being.

But he returned exactly in time for our next session. Still wearing his blue corduroys, he sauntered in as if nothing had happened. I shouted at him: "Where the hell have you been?"

"Newfoundland. Labrador. Greenland. Iceland."

"How did you get out of the hospital?"

"I just left."

"Without anyone seeing you?"

"That's right."

"How did you do that?"

"I told you—"

"With mirrors. Yes, I know." I also knew there was no sense in arguing the matter, and the tape at this point in the session is silent except for the distinct sound of my fingers tapping the arm of my chair. I finally said, "Next time tell me when you're going to leave."

"I did," he replied.

"And another thing: I don't think you should be telling the other patients you're going to take them back with you."

"I never said that to any of the patients."

"You didn't?"

"No. In fact I told them I can only take one person back with me."

"I don't think you should be making promises you can't keep."

"I have promised nothing." He bit into a huge strawberry from a bowlful brought in from her garden in Hoboken by Mrs. Trexler.

I was famished. My mouth was watering. This time I joined him. Chewing hungrily, we glared at each other for several minutes like prizefighters sizing up an opponent. "Tell me," I said. "If you can leave here any time you want, why do you stay?"

He swallowed a mouthful of berries, took a deep breath. "Well, it's as good a place as any to write my report, you feed me every day, and the fruit is wonderful. Besides," he added impishly, "I like you."

"Well enough to stay put for a while?"

"Until august seventeenth."

"Good. Now let's get started, shall we?"

"Certainly."

"All right. Can you draw a star map showing the night sky from anywhere in the galaxy? From Sirius, say?"

"No."

"Why not?"

"I have never been there."

"But you can do so for all the places you've been?"

"Naturally."

"Will you do a few of those for me before the next session?"

"No problem."

"Good. Now—where have you really been the past few days?"

"I told you: newfoundland, labrador—"

"Uh huh. And how are you feeling after your long journey?"

"Very well, thank you. And how have you been, narr?"

"Narr?"

"Gene, on K-PAX, is narr." It rhymed with "hair."

"I see. Is that from the French, meaning 'to confess'?"

"No, it is from the pax-o, meaning 'one who doubts.'"

"Oh. And what would 'prot' be in English—one who is cocksure?"

"Nope. 'Prot' is derived from an ancient K-PAXian word for 'sojourner.' Believe it or not by ripley."

"If I asked you to translate something from English to pax-o for me, something like *Hamlet,* for example, could you do it?"

"Of course. When would you like to have it?"

"Whenever you can get to it."

"Next week okay?"

"Fine. Now then. We've talked quite a bit about the sciences on K-PAX. Tell me about the arts on your planet."

"You mean painting and music? Stuff like that?"

"Painting, music, sculpture, dance, literature . . ."

The usual smile broke out, and the fingers came together. "It is similar in some ways to the arts on EARTH. But remember that we have had several billion years longer to develop them than you have. Our music is not based on anything as primitive as notes, nor any of our arts on subjective vision."

"Not based on notes? How else—"

"It is continuous."

"Can you give me an example?" With that he tore a sheet of paper from his little notebook and began to draw something on it.

While he did so I asked him why, with all his talents and capabilities, he needed to keep a written record of his observations. "Isn't it obvious?" he replied. "What if something happens to me before I get back to K-PAX?" He then showed me the following:

"This is one of my favorites. I learned it as a boy." As I tried to make sense out of the score, or whatever it was, he added, "You can see why I'm rather partial to your john cage."

"Can you hum a few bars of this thing?"

"You know I can't sing. Besides, it doesn't break down into 'tunes.' "

"May I keep this?"

"Consider it a souvenir of my visit."

"Thank you. Now. You said that your arts are not based on 'subjective vision.' What does that mean?"

"It means we don't have what you call 'fiction.' "

"Why not?"

"What is the point?"

"Well, through fiction, one often gains an understanding of truth."

"Why beat around the bush? Why not go right for the truth in the first place?"

"Truth means different things to different people."

"Truth is truth. What you are talking about is make-believe. Dream worlds. Tell me"—he bent over the notebook—"why do human beings have the peculiar impression that a belief is the same as the truth?"

"Because sometimes the truth hurts. Sometimes we need to believe in a better truth."

"What better truth can there be than truth?"

"There may be more than one kind of truth."

Prot continued to scribble in his notebook. "There is only one truth. Truth is absolute. You can't escape it, no matter how far you run." He said this rather wistfully, it seemed to me.

"There's another factor, too," I countered. "Our beliefs are based on incomplete and conflicting experiences. We need help to sort things out. Maybe you can help us."

He looked up in surprise. "How?"

"Tell me more about your life on K-PAX."

"What else would you like to know?"

"Tell me about your friends and acquaintances there."

"All K-PAXians are my friends. Except there is no word for 'friend' in pax-o. Or 'enemy.' "

"Tell me about some of them. Whoever comes to mind."

"Well, there is brot, and mano, and swon, and fled, and—"

"Who is brot?"

"He lives in the woods RILLward of reldo. Mano is—"

"Reldo?"

"A village near the purple mountains."

"And brot lives there?"

"In the woods."

"Why?"

"Because orfs usually live in the woods."

"What's an orf?"

"Orfs are something between our species and trods. Trods are much like your chimpanzees, only bigger."

"You mean orfs are subhuman?"

"Another of your famous contradictions in terms. But if you mean is he a forebear, the answer is yes. You see, we did not destroy our immediate progenitors as you did on EARTH."

"And you consider the orfs to be your friends?"

"Of course."

"What do you call your own species, by the way?"

"Dremers."

"And how many progenitors are there between trods and dremers?"

"Seven."

"And they are all still in existence on K-PAX?"

"Mais oui!"

"What are they like?"

"They are beautiful."

"Do you have to take care of them in some way?"

"Only clean up after them, sometimes. Otherwise they take care of themselves, as all beings do."

"Do they speak? Can you understand them?"

"Certainly. All beings 'speak.' You just have to know their language."

"Okay. Go on."

"Mano is quiet. She spends most of her time studying our insects. Swon is soft and green. Fled is—"

"Green?"

"Of course. Swon is an em. Something like your tree frogs, only they are as big as dogs."

"You call frogs by name?"

"How else would you refer to them?"

"Are you telling me you have names for all the frogs on K-PAX?"

"Of course not. Only the ones I know."

"You know a lot of lower animals?"

"They are not 'lower.' Just different."

"How do these species compare with those we have on Earth?"

"You have more variety, but, on the other hand, we have no carnivores. And," he beamed, "no flies, no mosquitoes, no cockroaches."

"Sounds too good to be true."

"Oh, it's true all right, believe me."

"Let's get back to the people."

"There are no 'people' on K-PAX."

"I meant the beings of your own species. The—uh—dremers."

"As you wish."

"Tell me more about your friend mano."

"I told you: She is fascinated by the behavior of the homs."

"Tell me more about her."

"She has soft brown hair and a smooth forehead and she likes to make things."

"Do you get along well with her?"

"Of course."

"Better than with other K-PAXians?"

106

"I get along well with everyone."

"Aren't there a few of your fellow dremers that you get along with—that you like—better than others?"

"I like all of them."

"Name a few."

That was a mistake. He named thirty-odd K-PAXians before I could stop him with: "Do you get along well with your father?"

"Really, gene, you've got to do something about that memory of yours. I can give you some tips if—"

"How about your mother?"

"Of course."

"Would you say you love her?"

"Love implies hate."

"You didn't answer my question."

"Love . . . like . . . it's all a matter of semantics."

"All right. Let me turn that around. Is there anyone you *don't* like? Is there anyone you actually *dis*like?"

"Everyone on K-PAX is just like me! Why would I hate anyone? Should I hate myself?"

"On Earth there are those who do hate themselves. Those who haven't lived up to their own standards or expectations. Those who have failed to achieve their goals. Those who have made disastrous mistakes. Those who have caused harm to someone and regretted it later on. . . ."

"I told you before—no one on K-PAX would cause harm to anyone else!"

"Not even unintentionally?"

"No!"

"Never?"

Yelling: "Are you deaf?"

"No. I hear you quite clearly. Please calm down. I'm sorry if I upset you." He nodded brusquely.

I knew I was onto something here, but I wasn't certain as to the best way to proceed. While he was composing himself we talked about some of the patients, including Maria and her protective alter egos—he seemed quite interested in her condition. Who knows where inspiration comes from? Or is it merely a momentary clearing in the fog of stupidity? In any case I realized at that moment that I had been focusing, perhaps for reasons of self-interest, on his delusion. What I should have been attacking was the hysterical amnesia! "Prot?"

His fists slowly unclenched. "What?"

"Something has occurred to me."

"Bully for you, doctor brewer."

"I was wondering whether you'd be willing to undergo hypnosis at our next session?"

"What for?"

"Let's call it an experiment. Sometimes hypnosis can call up recollections and feelings that are too painful to recall otherwise."

"I remember everything I have ever done. There is no need."

"Will you do it as a personal favor to me?" He eyed me suspiciously. "Why do you hesitate—are you afraid to be hypnotized?"

It was a cheap trick, but it worked. "Of course not!"

"Next Wednesday all right?"

"Next wednesday is the fourth of july. Do you work on your american holidays?"

"God, is it July already? All right. We'll test your susceptibility to the procedure next Tuesday, and begin the week after that. Does that suit you?"

Suddenly calm: "Perfectly, my dear sir."

"You're not planning on leaving again, are you?"

"I'll say it one more time: not until 3:31 A.M. on the seventeenth of august."

And he returned to Ward Two, where he was welcomed back like the prodigal son.

THE next morning Giselle was waiting at my office door when I arrived at the hospital. She was wearing the same outfit as before, or perhaps one of its clones. She was all tiny-tooth smiles. "Why didn't you tell me about prot?" she demanded.

I had stayed up until two o'clock to finish some editorial work, had come in early to prepare a speech for a Rotary Club luncheon, and was still distraught over prot's temporary disappearance. My office clock began to chime, further jangling my nerves and telling me what I didn't want to know. "What about him?" I snapped.

"I decided to make him the focus of the piece. With your permission, of course."

I dropped my bulging briefcase onto my desk. "Why prot?"

She literally fell into the brown leather chair and curled into the already familiar ball. I wondered whether this was premeditated or whether she was unaware of the charming effect it had on middle-aged men, especially those suffering from Brown's syndrome. I began to understand why she was such a successful reporter. "Because he fascinates me," she said.

"Did you know that he is my patient?"

"Betty told me. That's why I'm here. To see if you would let me look at his records." Her eyelids were fluttering like the wings of some exotic butterfly.

I busied myself with transferring the contents of my case to some logical place on the already overcrowded desk. "Prot is a special patient," I told her. "He requires very delicate treatment."

"I'll be careful. I wouldn't do anything that would jeopardize my own story. Or divulge any confidences," she added in a playful whisper. Then: "I know you're planning to write a book about him."

"Who told you that?" I practically shouted.

"Why, he—prot—told me."

"*Prot?* Who told *him?*"

"I don't know. But I want to assure you that my piece won't affect your book in any way. If anything, it should drum up some business for it. And I'll show it to you before I submit it for publication—how's that?" I stared at her for a moment, trying to think of some way out of this unwanted complication. She must have sensed my doubt. "I'll tell you what," she said. "If I can identify him for you, I get my story. Fair enough?" She had me and she knew it. "Plus any expenses I might incur," she added immediately.

O V E R the weekend I reviewed the transcripts of all eight sessions with prot. Everything pointed to at least one violent episode in his past that precipitated his hysterical "escape" from the real world, which he deeply hated, to a nonexistent, idyllic place where there are no human interactions to cause all the problems, large and small, that the rest of us have to live with every day. Nor the joys that make it all worthwhile . . .

I decided to ask prot to spend the Fourth of July at my home in order to see if a more or less normal family environment would bring anything out of him I hadn't seen before. I had done this with a few other patients, sometimes with beneficial results. My wife was in favor of the idea, even though I mentioned to her that prot may have been involved

110

in some sort of violent affair, and there was a possibility that—

"Don't be silly," she interrupted. "Bring him along."

How these things happen I haven't a clue, but by Monday morning everyone in Wards One and Two knew that prot was coming to the house for a barbecue. Almost every patient I ran into that day, including three of Maria's alters, who kept fastening buttons unfastened by other personalities, and vice versa, complained, good-naturedly, "You never invited *me* to your house, Dr. Brewer!" To every one of them I said, "You get well and get out of here, and I'll do exactly that." To which most of them replied, "I won't be here, Dr. Brewer. Prot is taking me with him!"

All but Russell, who had no intention of going to K-PAX: His place was on Earth. Indeed, with everyone in Wards One and Two enjoying a picnic on the hospital lawn, except for Bess, who stayed inside out of an imaginary rainstorm, Russ spent all of the Fourth in the catatonic ward, preaching the gospels. Unfortunately, none of those pathetic creatures jumped up and followed him out.

That same Monday morning Giselle was waiting for me again in her usual outfit, same piney bouquet. I asked her as politely as possible to please call Mrs. Trexler for an appointment whenever she wanted to see me. I started to tell her that I had patients to see, a lot of administrative work, papers to referee, letters to dictate and so on, but I had barely begun when she said, "I think I know how to track down your guy."

I said, "Come in."

Her idea was this: She wanted to have a linguist she knew listen to one of the interview tapes. This was one of those people who can pinpoint the area of the country where one was born and/or grew up, sometimes with uncanny accuracy. It is not based on dialect so much as phrasing—

whether you say "water fountain" or "bubbler," for example. It was a good suggestion, but impossible, of course, owing to patient/client privilege. She was ready for this. "Then can I tape a conversation with him myself?" I saw no compelling reason she should not, and told her I would ask Betty to arrange a time convenient for her and prot. "Never mind." She grinned slyly. "I've already done it." And she literally skipped away like a schoolgirl to get in touch with her expert. Her piney aura, however, stayed with me for the rest of the day.

Session Nine

I T was a beautiful Fourth of July: partly cloudy skies (I wonder why it's always in the plural—how many "skies" are there?), not too hot or humid, the air redolent of charcoal grills and freshly cut grass.

A holiday seems to generate a feeling of timelessness, bringing, as it does, blended memories of all those that came before. Even my father took the Fourth off and we always spent the day around the brick barbecue pit and the evening at the river watching the fireworks. I still live in my father's house, the one I grew up in, but we don't have to go anywhere now; we can see the nearby country club display right from our screened-in terrace. Even so, when the first Roman candle lights up the sky I invariably smell the river and the gunpowder and my father's Independence Day cigar.

I love that house. It's a big white frame with a patio as well as the second-story terrace, and the backyard is loaded with oaks and maples. The roots are deep. Right next door is the house my wife grew up in, and my old basketball coach still lives on the other side. I wondered, as I gathered up the sticks and leaves lying around the yard, whether any of my own children would be living here after we've gone, picking up loose twigs on the Fourth of July, thinking of me as I thought of my father. And I wondered whether similar thoughts might not have been buzzing around Shasta Daisy's head as she sniffed around her predecessor's little wooden marker barely visible in the back corner behind the grill—Daisy the Dog: 1967–1982.

By 2:00 the coals were heating up and the rest of my family began to arrive. First came Abby with Steve and the two boys, then Jennifer, who had brought her roommate, a dental student, from Palo Alto. Not a man, as we had thought, but a tall African-American woman wearing copper earrings the size of salad plates that hung down to and rested on her bare shoulders. And I do mean tall.

As soon as I saw Steve I told him about the variance between Charlie Flynn's description of the figure-eight orbit of K-PAX around its twin suns, and prot's version, which, if I understood it correctly, was more of a retrograde pattern, like that of a pendulum. Later I showed him the calendar and the second star chart prot had concocted—the one describing the sky as seen from K-PAX looking away from Earth. Steve shook his head in disbelief and drawled that Professor Flynn had just left for a vacation in Canada, but said he would mention all this to him when he got back. I asked him whether he knew of any physicists or astronomers who had disappeared in the last five years, particularly on August 17, 1985. To his knowledge there had been no such disappearances, though he joked that there were a few colleagues who he wished might quietly do so.

Freddy arrived from Atlanta, still wearing his airline uniform, alone as usual. Now everyone was here for the first time since Christmas. Chip, however, had better things to do and soon went off somewhere with his friends.

Just after that Betty showed up with her husband, an English professor at NYU, who happens to have a black belt in aikido. They had brought prot and one of our trainees, whom I had invited primarily because he had been an outstanding amateur wrestler and he, too, would be helpful in case prot showed any indication of turbulence. Shasta Daisy, extra nervous when so many people are present, barked at everyone who arrived from the safety of the underside of the back porch, her usual refuge.

Prot came bearing gifts: three more star maps representing the heavens as seen from various places he had "visited," as well as a copy of *Hamlet,* translated into pax-o. He hadn't been out of the car for five seconds, however, before an extraordinary thing happened. Shasta suddenly ran at him from the porch. I yelled, afraid she was going to attack him. But she stopped short, wagged her tail from ear to ear as only a Dalmatian can, and flattened herself against his leg. Prot, for his part, was down on the ground immediately, rolling and feigning with the dog, barking, even, and then they were up running all over the yard, my grandsons chasing along behind, Shakespeare and the charts blowing in the wind. Fortunately, we managed to recover all but the last page of the play.

After a while prot sat down on the grass and Shasta lay down beside him, bathing herself, utterly calm and content. Later, she played with Rain and Star for the very first time. Not once did she retreat to the porch the rest of that afternoon and evening, not even when the nearby country club celebration started off with a tremendous bang. She became a different dog that Fourth of July.

As, so to speak, did we all.

That night, after the fireworks were over and our guests had gone, Fred came into the family room downstairs, where I was shooting some pool and listening to *The Flying Dutchman* on our old hi-fi set.

For years I'd had the feeling that Fred wanted to tell me something. There had been times during pauses in conversations when I was sure he was trying to get something off his chest but couldn't quite bring himself to do it. I never tried to push him, figuring that when he was ready he would tell me or his mother what was bothering him.

That's not entirely true. I didn't press him because I was afraid he was going to tell us he was gay. It is something a father doesn't ordinarily want to hear—most fathers are heterosexual—and I'm sure his mother, who will not be satisfied with less than eight grandchildren, felt the same way.

Apparently motivated by a conversation with prot, Fred decided to come out with it. But it wasn't to tell me about his sexual orientation. The thing he had tried to bring up all those years, and couldn't, was his deep-seated fear of flying!

I have known dentists who quake at the sight of a drill and surgeons who are terrified to go under the knife. Sometimes that's why people get into those fields—it's a form of whistling in the dark. But I had never encountered an airline pilot who was afraid to fly. I asked him why on earth he had decided on that profession, and he told me this: I had mentioned at dinner years before that phobias could be treated by a gradual acclimation to the conditions that triggered them, and had given some examples, such as fear of snakes, of closets, and, yes, of flying. I had taken him with me to a conference near Disneyland when he was a boy, having no idea he was apprehensive about the flight. That was why he went to the airport the day after he graduated from high school and began to take flying lessons—to work out the problem on his

116

own. It didn't help, but he continued the training until he had soloed and flown cross-country and passed his flight test. Even after all that he was still afraid to fly. So he figured the only thing to do was to enroll in an aeronautical school and become a professional pilot. He obtained his commercial license, became an instructor, hauled canceled checks all over the Eastern seaboard, usually in the middle of the night and often in bad weather, and after a couple of years of that he was as horrified as ever at the prospect of leaving terra firma. Then he got his air transport "ticket," as he called it, and went to work for United Airlines. Now, five years later, after a brief conversation with prot, he had finally come to me for help.

We were a long time down in the family room, playing Ping-Pong and throwing darts and shooting pool as we talked. Nine years as a pilot and he still had nightmares about plunging to Earth from awesome heights, taking forever to fall through empty space, falling and falling and never reaching the ground.

I have had many patients, over a quarter century of practice, who were afraid of flying. For that matter, it is quite common among the general population, and for a very simple reason: Our ancestors were tree dwellers. As such, a fear of falling was of considerable evolutionary value—those who did not fall survived to reproduce. Most people are able to overcome this fear, at least functionally. On the other hand there are some who never go anywhere they can't get to by car or train or bus, no matter how inconvenient.

I explained all this to Fred and suggested that he very likely fell into the latter category.

He wanted to know what he should do.

I suggested he try some other line of work.

"That's exactly what prot said!" he cried, and for the first time in two decades, he hugged me. "But he thought I should talk to you about it first." I had never seen him so happy.

My sigh of relief turned out to be premature. Right after Freddy had gone, Jennifer came in, pink from a shower. She grabbed his cue stick, took a shot, missed. We talked a while about medical school, shooting all the while, until I noticed that she hadn't pocketed a single ball, which was unusual for her.

I said, "Is there something you wanted to talk to me about?"

"Yes, Daddy, there is." I knew it was something I didn't want to hear. She hadn't called me "Daddy" in years. And she had also been talking to prot.

But it sometimes takes Jenny a while to get to the point. "I saw you hugging Freddy," she said. "That was nice. I never saw you do that before."

"I wanted to lots of times."

"Why didn't you?"

"I don't know."

"Abby thinks you weren't much interested in our problems. She figured it was because you listened to other people's troubles all day long and didn't want to hear any more at home."

"I know. She told me tonight before she left. But it's not true. I care about all of you. I just didn't want you to think I was trying to interfere with your lives."

"Why not? Every other parent I know does."

"It's a long story."

She missed another easy shot. "Try me."

"Well, it's because of my father, mostly. Your grandfather."

"What did he do to you?"

"He wanted me to become a doctor."

"What's wrong with that?"

"I didn't want to be a doctor."

"Dad, how could he have made you go to med school? He died when you were eleven or twelve, didn't he?" Her voice cracked charmingly on "eleven" and "twelve."

"Yes, but he planted the seed and it kept growing. I couldn't seem to stop it. I felt guilty. I guess I wanted to finish the rest of his life for him. And I did it for my mother—your grandmother—too."

"I don't think you can live someone else's life for them, Dad. But if it's any consolation, I think you're a very good doctor."

"Thank you." I missed my next shot. "By the way, you didn't go to medical school because of me, did you?"

"Partly. But not because you wanted me to. If anything, I thought you didn't. You never took me to see your office or the rest of the hospital. Maybe that's why I became interested—it seemed so mysterious."

"I just didn't want to do to you what my father did to me. If I haven't told you before, I'm very happy you decided to become a doctor."

"Thank you, Dad." She studied the table for a long minute, then missed the next ball entirely, sinking the cue ball instead. "What else would you have done? If you hadn't gone into medicine, I mean?"

"I always wanted to be an opera singer."

At that she smiled the warm smile she inherited from her mother—the one that says: "How sweet."

That annoyed me a trifle. "What's the matter?" I said. "Don't you think I could have been a singer?"

"I think anyone should be anything he or she wants to

119

be," she replied, not smiling anymore. "That's what I wanted to talk to you about." With that she missed the twelveball by a mile.

"Shoot," I said.

"It's your turn."

"I mean, what's the problem?"

She threw herself into my arms and sobbed, "Oh, Daddy, I'm a lesbian!"

That was about midnight. I remember because Chip came in right afterward. He was acting strangely, too, and I braced myself for another revelation. Chip, however, had not talked to prot.

Even my grandsons behaved differently after that momentous Fourth of July. They stopped fighting and throwing things and began to bathe and to comb their hair without arguing about it—an almost miraculous change.

But back to the cookout. Prot wouldn't eat any of the chicken, but he consumed a huge Waldorf salad and a couple of gallons of various fruit juices, shouting something about "going for the gusto." He seemed quite relaxed, and played Frisbee and badminton with Rain and Star and Shasta all afternoon.

Then something happened. When Karen turned on the sprinkler so that the kids could cool off, prot, who appeared to be enjoying himself, suddenly became extremely agitated. He didn't turn violent, thank God, just stared for a moment in utter horror as Jennifer and the two boys splashed into and out of the spray. Suddenly he started screaming and running around the yard. I was thinking, "What the hell have I done?" when he stopped, dropped to his knees, and buried his face in his hands. Shasta was by his side in a second. Betty's husband and our trainee looked at me for instructions, but the only one I had was, "Turn off the goddamn sprinkler!"

I approached him cautiously, but before I could put a hand on his shoulder he raised his head, became as cheerful as ever, and started to frolic with Shasta again.

There were no further incidents that afternoon.

Karen and I had a lot to talk about that night and it was nearly dawn when we finally got to sleep. She wanted to know what Freddy would do after he left the airline, and she cried a little about Jenny—not because of her choice, but because she knew it was going to be difficult for her. Her last words before drifting off, however, were: "I hate opera."

GISELLE was waiting for me the next morning, jumping up and down, nearly beside herself. "He's from the Northwest!" she exclaimed. "Probably western Montana, northern Idaho, or eastern Washington!"

"That what your man said?"

"She's not a man, but that's what she said!"

"Wouldn't the police know if someone, especially a scientist, had disappeared from that part of the country five years ago?"

"They should. I know someone down at the Sixth Precinct. Want me to check for you?"

For the first time in several days I had to laugh. It appeared she knew someone in any line of work one could name. I threw up my arms. "Sure, why not, go ahead." She was out the door like a shot.

That same morning, Betty, wearing an enormous pair of copper earrings in another desperate attempt to get pregnant, I presumed, brought in a stray kitten. She had found it in the subway station, and I assumed she was going to take it home with her that evening. But instead she suggested that we let the patients take care of it.

The presence of small animals in nursing and retirement

homes has proven to be of great benefit to the residents, providing badly needed affection and companionship and generally bolstering their spirits to such a degree that life spans are actually increased significantly. The same may be true for the population at large. To my knowledge, however, such a program had not been introduced in mental institutions.

After due consideration—we are an experimental hospital, after all—I asked Betty to instruct the kitchen staff to see that the kitten was fed regularly, and decided to let it roam Wards One and Two to see what would happen.

It headed straight for prot.

A short time later, after he had nuzzled it for a while and "spoken" to it, it went out to meet the other inhabitants of its new world.

One or two of the patients, notably Ernie and several of Maria's alters, stayed away from it, for reasons of their own. But most of the others were delighted with it. I was especially surprised and gratified to see that Chuck the curmudgeon took to it immediately. "Doesn't stink a bit," he averred. He spent hours tempting it with bits of string and a small rubber ball someone had found on the grounds. Many of the other patients joined in. One of these, to my amazement, was Mrs. Archer, who, I discovered, had owned numerous cats before coming to MPI.

But the most remarkable effect of the kitten was on Bess. Unable to sustain a relationship with another human being, she became totally devoted to "La Belle Chatte." She assumed the responsibility for feeding her and emptying her litter box and taking her for romps on the grounds. If anyone else wanted to play with the kitten, Bess immediately gave her up, of course, with a wise, sad nod, as if to say, "You're right—I don't deserve to have her anyway." But when night came, La Belle invariably sought out Bess, and the staff would find them in the mornings sharing the same pillow.

After a few days of this I began to wonder whether another kitten or two might not have an even greater salutary effect on the patients. I decided to get a tomcat later on and let nature take its course.

Session Ten

T HERE are two probes available for penetrating the carapace of hysterical amnesia; each has its proponents, each has its place. The first is sodium pentothal, also called "truth serum." A reasonably safe treatment, it has met with some success in difficult cases, and is favored by many of our own staff, including Dr. Villers. Hypnosis, in experienced hands, offers the same possibilities, but without the potential risk of side effects. With either method events long forgotten are often recalled with amazingly vivid clarity.

When I learned hypnosis as a resident many years ago I was skeptical about its value in psychiatric evaluation and treatment. But it has begun to come into its own in recent years, and is the method of choice in the management of many psychopathologies. Of course, as with other methods, success depends not only on the skill of the practitioner but also, to a great degree, on the disposition of the patient. Thus, the hypnotizability of the subject is routinely determined before treatment is initiated.

The Stanford test is used most often for this assessment. It takes less than an hour and provides a measure of the patient's ability to concentrate, his responsiveness, imagination, and willingness to cooperate. Subjects are rated on a scale of zero to twelve, the higher numbers indicating the greatest hypnotic susceptibility. Psychiatric patients, as well as the general public, average about seven on this test. I have known a few tens. Prot obtained a score of twelve.

My purpose in using hypnosis in prot's case was to uncover the traumatic event which had led to his hysterical amnesia and delusion. When had this incident occurred? My best guess was August 17, 1985, approximately four years and eleven months earlier.

The plan was simple enough: to take prot back to his childhood and carefully bring him up to the time of the putative traumatic event. In this way I hoped not only to determine the circumstances that led to whatever catastrophe had apparently befallen him, but also to get some information on the background and character of my patient.

PROT seemed to be in good spirits when he arrived in my examining room and, while he went to work on a pomegranate, we chatted about Waldorf salads and the infinite number of possible combinations of fruit juices. When he had finished his snack I turned on the tape recorder and asked him to relax.

"I am completely relaxed," he replied.

"Good. All right. I'd like you to focus your attention on that little white spot on the wall behind me." He did this. "Just stay relaxed, breathe deeply, in and out, slowly, in and out, good. Now I'm going to count from one to five. As the numbers increase you will find yourself becoming more and more drowsy, your eyelids becoming heavier and heavier. By the time I get to five you will be in a deep sleep, but you will be able to hear everything I say. Understand?"

"Of course. My beings didn't raise no dummies."

"Okay, let's begin now. One . . ."

Prot was a textbook subject, one of the best I ever had. By the count of three his eyes were tightly closed. On four his breathing had slowed and his facial expression had become completely blank. On five his pulse rate was forty bpm (I was beginning to be concerned—sixty-five was normal for him—though he looked okay) and he made no response when I coughed loudly.

"Can you hear me?"

"Yes."

"Raise your arms over your head." He complied with this request. "Now lower them." His hands dropped into his lap. "Good. Now I'm going to ask you to open your eyes. You will remain in a deep sleep, but you will be able to see me. Now—open your eyes!" Prot's eyes blinked open. "How do you feel?"

"Like nothing."

"Good. That's exactly how you *should* feel. All right. We are going back in time now; it is no longer the present. You are becoming younger. Younger and younger. You are a young man, younger still, now an adolescent, and still you are becoming younger. Now you are a child. I want you to recall the earliest experience you can remember. Think hard. What do you see?"

Without hesitation: "I see a casket. A silver casket with a blue lining."

My own heart began to beat faster. "Whose casket is it?"

"A man's."

"Who is the man?" The patient hesitated for a moment. "Don't be afraid. You can tell me."

"It is the father of someone I know."

"A friend's father?"

"Yes." Prot's words came out rather slowly and sing-songy, as though he were five or six years old.

"Is your friend a boy or girl?"

Prot squirmed around in his chair. "A boy."

"What is his name?"

No response.

"How old is he?"

"Six."

"How old are *you*?"

No response.

"What is *your* name?"

No response.

"Do you live in the same town as the other boy?"

Prot rubbed his nose with the back of his hand. "No."

"You are visiting him?"

"Yes."

"Are you a relative?"

"No."

"Where do you live?"

No response.

"Do you have any brothers or sisters?"

"No."

"Does your friend have any brothers or sisters?"

"Yes."

"How many?"

"Two."

"Brothers or sisters?"

"Sisters."

"Older or younger?"

"Older."

"What happened to their father?"

"He died."

"Was he sick?"

"No."

"Did he have an accident?"

"Yes."

"He was killed in an accident?"

"No."

"He was hurt and died later?"

"Yes."

"Was it a car accident?"

"No."

"Was he injured at work?"

"Yes."

"Where did he work?"

"At a place where they make meat."

"A slaughterhouse?"

"Yes."

"Do you know the name of the slaughterhouse?"

"No."

"Do you know the name of the town your friend lives in?"

No response.

"What happened after the funeral?"

"We went home."

"What happened after that?"

"I don't remember."

"Can you remember anything else that happened that day?"

"No, except I got knocked over by a big, shaggy dog."

"What is the next thing you remember?"

Prot sat up a little straighter and stopped squirming. Otherwise there was little change in his demeanor. "It is night. We are in the house. He is playing with his butterfly collection."

"The other boy?"

"Yes."

"And what are you doing?"

"Watching him."

"Do you collect butterflies too?"

"No."

"Why are you watching him?"

"I want him to come outside."

"Why do you want him to come outside?"

"To look at the stars."

"Doesn't he want to go?"

"No."

"Why not?"

"It reminds him of his father. He'd rather mess with his stupid butterflies."

"But you'd rather look at the stars."

"Yes."

"Why do you want to look at the stars?"

"I live there."

"Among the stars?"

"Yes." I remember my initial discouragement at hearing this answer. It seemed to mean that prot's delusion had begun extremely early in life; so early, perhaps, as to preclude a determination of its causative events. But suddenly I understood! Prot was a secondary personality, whose primary was the boy whose father had died when he was six!

"What is your name?"

"Prot."

"Where do you come from?"

"From the planet K-Pax."

"Why are you here?"

"He wanted me to come."

"Why did he want you to come?"

"He calls me when something bad happens."

"Like when his father died."

"Yes."

"Did something bad happen today?"

"Yes."

"What happened?"

"His dog was run over by a truck."

"And that's when he called you."

"Yes."

"How does he do that? How does he call you?"

"I don't know. I just sorta know it."

"How did you get to Earth?"

"I don't know. I just came." Prot hadn't yet "developed" light travel in his mind!

"How old is your friend now?"

"Nine."

"What year is it?"

"Nineteen—uh—sixty-six."

"Can you tell me your friend's name now?"

No response.

"He has a name, doesn't he?"

Prot stared blankly at the spot on the wall behind me. I was about to go on when he said, "It's a secret. He doesn't want me to tell you." But now I knew he was in there somewhere and prot, apparently, could consult with him.

"Why doesn't he want you to tell me?"

"If I tell you, something bad will happen."

"I promise you nothing bad will happen. Tell him I said that."

"All right." Pause. "He still doesn't want me to tell you."

"He doesn't have to tell me right now if he doesn't want to. Let's go back to the stars. Do you know where K-Pax is in the sky?"

"Up there." He pointed. "In the constellation Lyra."

"Do you know the names of all the constellations?"

"Most of them."

"Does your friend know the constellations too?"

"He used to."

"Has he forgotten them?"

"Yes."

"Is he no longer interested in them?"

"No."

"Why not?"

"His father died."

"His father taught him about the stars?"

"Yes."

"He was an amateur astronomer?"

"Yes."

"Was his father always interested in the stars?"

"No."

"When did he become interested in them?"

"After he was hurt at work."

"Because he had nothing to do?"

"No. He couldn't sleep."

"Because of the pain?"

"Yes."

"Did he sleep during the day?"

"Only one or two hours."

"I see. And one of the constellations your friend's father told him about was Lyra?"

"Yes."

"When?"

"Just before he died."

"When he was six?"

"Yes."

"Did he ever tell him there were planets around any of the stars in Lyra?"

"He said there were probably planets around a lot of the stars in the sky."

"One more thing. Why don't you go out and watch the stars by yourself?"

"I can't."

"Why not?"

"He wants me to stay with him." Prot yawned. He was beginning to sound tired. I didn't want to push him too far at this point.

"I think that's enough for one day. You may close your eyes. I'm going to start counting backwards now, from five to one. As I count you will become more and more alert. On the count of one you will be wide awake, refreshed, and feeling fine. Five . . . four . . . three . . . two . . . one." I snapped my fingers.

Prot looked at me and smiled brightly. "When do we begin?" he said.

"It's already over."

"Ah. The old 'fastest gun in the west' routine."

"I know that feeling!"

He had his notebook out; he wanted me to tell him how hypnosis worked. I spent the rest of the hour trying to explain something I didn't fully understand myself. He seemed a little disappointed.

After Jensen and Kowalski had escorted him back to the wards I listened to the tape of the session we had just completed and, with mounting excitement, jotted down my conclusions. It seemed clear to me that prot was a dominant secondary personality who had come into being as a result of the perhaps unexpected death of his alter ego's father, a trauma which was obviously too much for the primary personality to bear. It seemed evident also why he (prot) had chosen an alien existence: His (their) father had instigated in him an interest in the stars and in the possibility of extraterrestrial life occurring among them, and this revelation had come immediately prior to his father's demise.

But this did not account for the extraordinary dominance of prot over the primary personality. It is the secondary identity who ordinarily remains in the background, watching, waiting to take over when the host personality runs into difficulty. My guess was that some far more traumatic event must have drawn the primary—let's call him Pete—into a thick, protective shell, from which he rarely, if ever, ventured. And I was more certain than ever that this terrible incident, whatever it was, occurred on August 17, 1985, the date of prot's most recent "arrival" on Earth. Or perhaps a day or two earlier, if it had taken a while for Pete to "call" prot, or for him to respond.

Why did I not suspect that prot was a secondary personality earlier on? MPD is not an easy diagnosis under the best of circumstances, and prot never showed any of the symptoms usually associated with this disorder: headaches, mood changes, a variety of physical ailments, depression. Except, possibly, for his outbursts of anger in sessions six and eight, and the episode of panic on the Fourth of July, the host personality (Pete) had never made his presence felt. Finally, I was completely thrown off by his other aberrant traits—a dominant secondary personality who is himself delusional, and a savant as well—the odds against such a phenomenon must be astronomical!

But who was Pete, the primary personality? Apparently he was in there somewhere, living the life of a recluse in his own body, refusing to divulge his name or much of his background, except that he was born in 1957, apparently, to a slaughterhouse worker who died in 1963, perhaps somewhere in the northwestern part of the United States, and he had a mother and two older sisters. Not much to go on, but it might help the police trace his origin. Strictly speaking, it was Pete's identity, rather than prot's, that we needed to ascertain. Any information we could get about him, any knowledge of things familiar to him, might facilitate my persuading him to come out.

All this put prot's "departure date" into an entirely new light. It is one thing for a patient to announce an end to a delusion, but quite another for a dominant alter to disappear, leaving behind a hysteric, or maybe worse. If prot were to leave before I could get to Pete, it might well preclude my ever being able to help him at all.

I wondered whether the *un*hypnotized prot knew anything about Pete. If not, the plan would remain as before: to bring prot/Pete slowly and carefully, under hypnosis, up to the time of the traumatic event(s) which precipitated Pete's dramatic withdrawal from conscious existence. Even if he did know about Pete, however, hypnosis might still be necessary, both to facilitate prot's recollection and to make possible direct contact with the host personality.

But there was a dilemma associated with this approach. On the one hand, I needed to talk to Pete as soon as possible. On the other, forcing him to relive that terrible moment prematurely could be devastating, and cause him to withdraw even further into his protective shell.

★　★　★

GISELLE seemed a little less cheerful than usual the following Monday morning. "My friend down at the Sixth Precinct couldn't find any report of a missing person who disappeared from the upper West in August of 1985," she said, consulting a little red notebook much like the one prot was fond of. "Somebody killed a man and then himself in a little town in Montana on the sixteenth of that month, and in Boise on the eighteenth another guy ran off with his secretary and one hundred fifty thousand dollars of his company's funds. But your guy isn't dead, and the one who ran off with his secretary is still in the Idaho State Penitentiary. My friend is expanding the search to cover January through July of 1985, and then all of the United States and Canada. It will be a while before he gets the results.

"I also know someone in the Research Library at New York Public; during her breaks she's doing some searches for me for the week of August seventeenth. You know—newspaper reports of anything unusual that might have happened during that period in Montana, Idaho, Washington, and Oregon. Nothing there so far, either." She closed the little book. "Of course," she added, "he might have been raised in the Northwest and then moved somewhere else. . . ."

I told her about prot's (Pete's) father and the slaughterhouse. "Ha!" she replied. "I wonder how many of those things there are in the United States?"

"I don't know."

"I'll find out," she said with a wave.

"Wait a minute," I called after her. "He was born in 1957."

"How did you find this stuff out?" she demanded to know.

"Ve haff arrrr vays, mein Mädchen."

She ran back and kissed me on the mouth (almost) before dashing out. I felt about thirteen years old again.

KAREN and I were inseparable after my father's funeral. If we could've lived together, we would have. I especially loved her fat, pink cheeks, which became red and shiny, like little apples, in the wintertime. But it took me another year to get up the nerve to kiss her.

I studied the way they did it in the movies, practiced for months on the back of my hand. The problem was, I wasn't sure she wanted me to. Not that she turned away whenever our faces were close together, but she never indicated in any clear way that she was interested. Finally I decided to do it. With all those movies it seemed abnormal not to.

We were sitting on the sofa at her house reading Donald Duck comics, and I had been thinking about it all morning. I knew you were supposed to kiss sort of sideways so your noses wouldn't bang together, and when she turned toward me to show me Donald's nephews carrying picket signs reading: "Unca Donald is stewped," I made my move. I missed, of course, as first kisses often do, as Giselle's did before she ran out.

THAT afternoon I found Giselle in the exercise room talking animatedly with prot. La Belle was asleep in his lap. Both were jotting things down in their respective notebooks, and prot seemed quite comfortable with her. I didn't have time to join them, but she told me later some of the things they had discussed. For instance, they had been comparing the Earth with K-PAX, and one of the questions she had asked him, in a brash attempt to track down my patient's origins, was where he would like to live if he could live anywhere on Earth. She was hoping he would say "Olympia, Washington," or some such town in the upper West. Instead, he answered, "sweden."

"Why Sweden?" she wanted to know.

"Because it's the country most like K-PAX."

The subject then turned to those human beings who seemed most like K-PAXians to him. Here is what he said: Henry Thoreau, Mohandas Gandhi, Albert Schweitzer, John Lennon, and Jane Goodall.

"Can you imagine a world full of Schweitzers?" she hooted.

I said, "John Lennon?"

"Have you ever heard 'Imagine'?"

I told her I would look it up.

Then she said something I had been wondering myself: "You know what else? I think he can talk to animals!"

I said I wasn't surprised.

I had no time for them that afternoon because I was on my way to Ward Four, where Russell was trying to get in. Apparently distraught with the loss of his followers to prot's counsel and advice, and his failure to wake up the catatonic patients, he had decided to convert some of the psychopaths. When I arrived I found the nurses attempting to get him to go back to his own ward. He was up on his toes shouting through the little barred window high in the steel door, "Take heed that no man deceiveth you! For many shall cometh in my name, saying, I am the Christ; and shall deceiveth many!" Apparently his words were not falling on deaf ears, as I could hear laughter coming from inside. But he kept on yelling, even after I pleaded with him to go back to Ward Two. I ordered a shot of Thorazine and had him taken back to his room.

That same day two other things happened that I should have paid more attention to. First, I got a report that Howie had asked one of the residents how to perform a tracheotomy. Dr. Chakraborty finally told him, thinking Howie was going to show Ernie how easily he could be saved even if he were to get choked on something, despite the unfortunate example of his mother's demise.

The other event concerned Maria. One of her alters, a sultry female called Chiquita, somehow got into Ward Three and, before anyone discovered her presence there, offered herself to Whacky. But the results were the same as with the prostitute prescribed earlier. Facing this unexpected rejection, Chiquita quickly exited and Maria appeared. Though finding herself with a naked man engaged in self-manipulation she didn't become hysterical, as you might expect. Rather, she immediately began to pray for Whacky, whose despair she seemed to understand completely!

On the lighter side, Chuck presented prot with a drawing summarizing his assessment of the human race, one of many attempts, I discovered, to impress prot so that he would take Chuck to K-PAX with him. It is reproduced here:

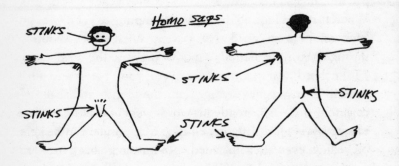

Purely by coincidence this diagram described almost perfectly our second applicant for the position of permanent director. He obviously had not bathed in weeks or even months. A blizzard of dandruff snowed from his head and drifted onto his shoulders. His teeth seemed to be covered with lichen. And, like the previous candidate, Dr. Choate, who checked his fly every few minutes, the man came with excellent references.

Session Eleven

I had been gazing out my office window at a croquet match on the lawn below just before prot came in for his next interview. I nodded toward the fruit basket and asked him what sorts of games he had played as a boy. "We don't have games on K-PAX," he replied. "We don't need them. Nor what you call 'jokes,'" he added, scrutinizing a dried fig. "I've noticed that human beings laugh a lot, even at things that aren't funny. I was puzzled by this at first until I understood how sad your lives really are."

I was sorry I had asked.

"By the way, this fig has a pesticide residue on it."

"How do you know that?"

"I can see it."

"*See* it? Oh." I had forgotten about his ultraviolet vision. With time at a premium, I nonetheless could not resist the opportunity to ask him what our world looked like from his perspective. In response, he spent nearly fifteen minutes trying to describe an incredibly beautiful visage of vibrantly colored flowers, birds, and even ordinary rocks, which lit up like gems for him. The sky itself took on a shimmering, bright, violet aura through his eyes. It appeared that prot's vista was tantamount to being permanently high on one or another psychedelic drug. I wondered whether van Gogh had not enjoyed a similar experience.

He had put down the offensive fig while he expounded on his exceptional faculty, and found one more to his liking. While he masticated I carefully proceeded. "Last time, under hypnosis, you told me about a friend of yours, an Earth being, and his father's death, and his butterfly collection, and some other things. Do you remember any of that now?"

"No."

"Well, did you have such a friend?"

"Yes."

"Is he still a friend of yours?"

"Of course."

"Why didn't you tell me about him before?"

"You never asked."

"I see. Where is he now, do you know?"

"He is waiting. I am going to take him back to K-PAX with me. That is, if he still wants to go. He vacillates a lot."

"And where is your friend waiting?"

"He is in a safe place."

"Do you know where that is?"

"Certainly."

"Can you tell me?"

"Nay, nay."

"Why not?"

"Because he asked me not to tell anyone."

"Can you at least tell me his name?"

"Sorry."

Given the circumstances, I decided to take a chance. "Prot, I'm going to tell you something you may find hard to believe."

"Nothing you humans come up with surprises me anymore."

"You and your friend are the same person. That is, you and he are separate and distinct identities of the same person."

He seemed genuinely shocked. "That is patently absurd."

"It's true."

Annoyed now, but under control: "Is that another of those 'beliefs' that passes for truth with your species?"

It had been a long shot, and it had missed. There was no way to prove the contention and no point in wasting any more time. When he had finished his snack I asked if he was ready to be hypnotized again. He nodded suspiciously, but by the time I had counted to three he was already "gone."

I began: "Last time you told me about your Earth friend, beginning with his father's death. Do you remember?"

"Yes." Prot was trance anamnestic—he could remember previous hypnotic sessions, but only while in the hypnotic state.

"Good. Now I want you to think back once again, but not so far back as last time. You and your friend are high school seniors. Twelfth-graders. What do you see?"

At this point prot slouched down in his chair, fiddled with his nails, and began to chew on an imaginary piece of gum. "I was never a high school senior," he said. "I never went to school."

"Why not?"

"We don't have schools on K-PAX."

"What about your friend? Does he go to school?"

"Yes, he does, the dope. I couldn't talk him out of it."

"Why would you want to talk him out of it?"

"Are you kidding? Schools are a total waste of time. They try to teach you a bunch of crap."

"Like what?"

"Like how great america is, better than any other country, how you have to have wars to protect your 'freedoms,' all kinds of junk like that."

"Does your friend feel the same way you do about that?"

"Nah. He believes all that garbage. They all do."

"Is your friend there with you now?"

"Yes."

"Can he hear us?"

"Of course. He's right here."

"May I speak with him?"

Again the momentary hesitation. "He doesn't want to."

"If he changes his mind, will you let me know?"

"I guess."

"Will he tell me his name, at least?"

"No way."

"Well, we have to call him something. How about Pete?"

"That's not his name, but okay."

"All right. Is he a senior now?"

"Yep."

"What year is it?"

"Nineteen seventy-four."

"How old are you?"

"A hunnert and seventy-seven."

"And how old is Pete?"

"Seventeen."

"Does he know you come from K-PAX?"

"Yes."

143

"How does he know that?"

"I told him."

"What was his reaction to that?"

"He thinks it's cool."

"Incidentally, how did you learn to speak English so well? Did he teach you?"

"Nah. It's not very difficult. You should try speaking w:xljqzs/k..mns pt."

"Where did you land when you came to Earth?"

"You mean this trip?"

"Yes."

"China."

"Not Zaire?"

"Why should I land in zaire when china was pointing toward K-PAX?"

"Do you have any other Earth friends? Is there anyone else there with you?"

"Nobody here but us chickens."

"How many chickens are you?"

"Just me and him."

"Tell me more about Pete. What's he like?"

"What's he like? He's all right. Kinda quiet. Keeps to himself. He's not as smart as I am, but that doesn't matter on EARTH."

"No? And what does matter?"

"All that matters is that you're a 'nice guy,' and not too bad looking."

"And is he?"

"I suppose."

"Can you describe him?"

"Yes."

"Please do."

"He's beginning to wear his hair long. He has brown

eyes, medium complexion, and twenty-eight pimples, which he puts Clearasil on all the time."

"Are his eyes sensitive to bright light?"

"Not particularly. Why should they be?"

"What makes him a nice guy?"

"He smiles a lot, he helps the dumber kids with their assignments, he volunteers to set up the bleachers for the home games, stuff like that. He's vice-president of the class. Everybody likes him."

"You sound as though you're not so sure they should."

"I know him better than anybody else."

"And you think he's not as nice as everybody thinks."

"He's not as nice as he makes out."

"In what way?"

"He has a temper. It gets out of hand sometimes."

"What happens when it gets out of hand?"

"He gets mad. Throws things around, kicks inanimate objects."

"What makes him mad?"

"Things that seem unfair, that he can't do anything about. You know."

I was pretty sure I did know. It had something to do with the helplessness and anger he felt at the time of his father's death. "Can you give me an example?"

"One time he found a kid beating up on a smaller kid. The older guy was a big redheaded bully and everybody hated him. He had broken the other kid's glasses, and his nose, too, I think. My friend beat the shit out of him. I tried to stop him but he wouldn't listen."

"What happened then? Was the bully badly hurt? Did he try to get even later on?"

"He lost a couple teeth is all. He was mostly afraid my friend would tell everybody what happened. When he didn't, and asked the little kid not to either, they became the best of buddies. All three of them."

"What do these other guys think about you?"

"They don't know about me."

"Does anyone besides your friend know about you?"

"Nary a soul."

"All right. Back to your friend. Does this anger of his show itself often?"

"Not very. Hardly ever at school."

"Does he ever get mad at his mother and sisters?"

"Never. He doesn't see his sisters much. They're already married and gone. One of them moved away."

"Tell me about his mother."

"She's nice. She works at the school. At the cafeteria. She doesn't make much money, but she does a lot of gardening and canning. They have enough to eat, but not much else. She's still trying to pay back all of his dad's doctor bills."

"Where do they live? I mean is it a house? What kind of neighborhood is it in?"

"It's a small three-bedroom house. It looks like all the others on the street."

"What sorts of things does your friend do for entertainment? Movies? Books? Television?"

"There's only one movie theater in town. They have an old tv set that doesn't work half the time. My friend reads a lot, and he also likes to walk around in the woods."

"Why?"

"He wants to be a biologist."

"What about his grades?"

"What about them?"

"Does he get good grades?"

"A's and b's. He should do better. He sleeps too much."

"What are his best subjects?"

146

"He's pretty good in latin and science. Not so hot in english and math."

"Is he a good athlete?"

"He's on the wrestling team."

"Is he planning to go to college?"

"He was until a few days ago."

"What happened? Is there a problem?"

"Yes."

"Is that why he called you?"

"Yes."

"Does he call you often now?"

"Once in a while."

"And what is the problem? Money? There are scholarships available, or—"

"It's more complicated than that."

"How so?"

"He has a girlfriend."

"And she doesn't want him to go?"

"It's more complicated than that."

"Can you tell me about it?"

After a brief pause, possibly for consultation with his "friend": "She's pregnant."

"Oh, I see."

"Happens all the time."

"And he feels he has to marry her?"

"Unfortunately." He shrugged.

" 'Unfortunately' because he won't be able to go to college?"

"That and the religion problem."

"What's the religion problem?"

"She's a catholic."

"You don't like Catholics?"

"It's not that I dislike catholics, or any other group defined by its superstitious beliefs. It's that I know what's going to happen."

"What's going to happen?"

"He's going to settle down in this company town that killed his father and he's going to have a bunch of kids that nobody will associate with because their mother is a catholic."

"Where is this town?"

"I told you—he doesn't want me to tell you that."

"I thought he might have changed his mind."

"When he makes up his mind about something, nobody can change it."

"He sounds pretty strong-willed."

"About some things."

"What, for example?"

"About her."

"Who—his girlfriend?"

"Yep."

"I may be dense, but I still don't see why her being a Catholic is such a serious problem."

"That's because you don't live here. Her family lives on the wrong side of the tracks. Literally."

"Maybe they will be able to overcome the problem."

"How?"

"She could change her faith. They could move away."

"Not a chance. She's too attached to her family."

"Do you hate her?"

"Me? I don't hate anyone. I hate the chains people shackle themselves with."

"Like religion."

"Religion, family responsibilities, having to make a living, all that stuff. It's so *stifling*, don't you think?"

"Sometimes. But they're things we have to learn to live with, aren't they?"

"Not me!"

"Why not?"

"We don't have all that crap on K-PAX."

"Will you be going back there soon?"

"Any time now."

"How long do you usually stay on Earth?"

"Depends. A few days, usually. Just long enough to help him over the rough spots."

"All right. Now listen carefully. I'm going to ask you to come forward in time several days. Let's say two weeks. Where are you now?"

"On K-PAX."

"Good. What do you see?"

"A forest with lots of soft places to lie down on, and fruit trees, and all kinds of other beings wandering around. . . ."

"Much like the kind of forest your friend enjoys hiking in?"

"Something like that, but nobody is bulldozing it down to build a shopping center."

"Tell me about some of the plants and animals in the woods there on K-PAX." I was curious to find out whether the young prot had a fully developed concept of his home planet, or whether that came later. While he was describing the flora and fauna I retrieved his file and pulled out the information that prot had divulged to me in sessions five through eight. I quizzed him on the names of grains, fruits and vegetables, the various animal "beings," even about light travel and the K-PAXian calendar. I won't repeat the questions and answers here, but they confirmed my suspicion that the creation of his alien world was developed over many years. For example, he could tell me the names of only six grains at this stage.

Our time ran out just as prot decided to make a trip to one of the K-PAXian libraries. He asked me whether I would like to join him. I said I was sorry, I had some appointments.

"It's your loss," he said.

After I had awakened him, and before he left my examining room, I asked prot whether he could, in fact, talk to animals, as Giselle and I suspected.

"Of course," he replied.

"Can you communicate with all our beings?"

"I have a little difficulty with homo sapiens."

"Can you talk to dolphins and whales?"

"They're beings, aren't they?"

"How do you do that?"

He wagged his head in abject frustration. "You humans consider yourselves the smartest of the EARTH beings. Am I right?"

"Yes."

"Then obviously the other beings speak much simpler languages than yours, right?"

"Well—"

Out came the notebook, pencil poised. "So if you're so smart, and their languages are so simple, how come you can't communicate with them?" He waited for an answer. Unfortunately, I didn't have one.

JUST before I left for the day Giselle gave me another discouraging report from the police. Her contact had come up with a list of all disappearances, during the last ten years, of white males born between 1950 and 1965 in the entire United States and Canada. There had been thousands during this period, of course, but not a single one even came close to matching prot's profile. Some were too tall, some were bald, some were blue-eyed, some were dead, some had been found and were accounted for. Unless prot were a female in disguise, was much older or younger than he seemed, or someone whose disappearance had not been noticed, our patient, for all practical purposes, did not exist.

She was also waiting for the names and locations of all the slaughterhouses operating anywhere in North America between 1974 and 1985.

"You can eliminate the ones in or near large cities," I told her. "There's only one movie theater."

She nodded her acknowledgment. She looked tired. "I'm going to go home and sleep for about two days," she said, yawning. How I wished I could have done the same!

I was lying awake that night trying to make some sense of the day's events—why, I wondered hazily, was there no record of Pete's disappearance? And what good, I tried to reason, was a list of slaughterhouses without further information as to where our abattoir might be located?—when I got a call from Dr. Chakraborty. Ernie was in the clinic. Someone had tried to kill him!

"What? Who?" I barked.

"Howie!" came the chilling reply.

All I could think of as I sped down the expressway was: Jesus Christ! What have I done? Whatever happened to Ernie was my fault, my responsibility, just as I was responsible for everything else that happened at the hospital. It was one of the worst moments of my life. But even at that blackest of hours I was heartened by the glow of the city, her throbbing lights bright against the steel-gray background of the dawning sky, as full of defiant life as the night, some forty years earlier, that we futilely rushed my father to the hospital. Same glowing sky, same darkening guilt.

Ernie was still in the emergency room when I got to MPI. Dr. Chakraborty met me in the corridor with: "You are not to worry. He is very fine." And indeed he was sitting up in bed, sans mask, smiling, his hands behind his head.

"How are you feeling, Ernie?"

"Wonderful. Absolutely wonderful." I had never seen a smile quite like his. It was positively beatific.

"What happened, for God's sake?"

"My good friend Howie just about strangled me to death." When he threw his head back to laugh, I could see a red abrasion where something had been wrapped around his neck. "That old son-of-a-bitch. I love him."

"Love him? He tried to kill you!"

"No he didn't. He made me *think* he tried to kill me. Oh, it was fantastic. I was asleep. You know, with my hands tied and everything? He wrapped something around my neck—a handkerchief or something—and tightened it up, and there wasn't a damn thing I could do about it."

"Go on."

"When I stopped breathing and became unconscious he somehow lifted me onto a gurney and ran me up here to the infirmary. They got me going again in a hurry, and when I woke up I realized immediately what he had done."

"What do you think he did?" I remember saying to myself as I asked him this: I must be a psychiatrist! It was all I could do not to laugh.

"He taught me a lesson I'll never forget."

"Which was?"

"That dying is nothing to fear. In fact, it's quite pleasant."

"How so?"

"Well, you've heard that old adage—when you die your life passes before your eyes? Well, it does! But only the good parts! In my case, I was a child again. It was wonderful! My mother was there, and my dog, and I had all my old toys and games and my catcher's mitt. . . . It was just like living my whole childhood over again! But it was no dream. It was really happening! All those memories—I never realized what a wonderful thing childhood is until I got the chance to relive it like that. And then, when I was nine, it started all over again! And again! Over and over again! It was the best thing that ever happened to me!" There he was, his skin pale as a scallop, laughing about the event whose prospect had terrified him all his life. "I can hardly wait for the real thing!"

They had taken Howie to Ward Four. I let him stew there the rest of that day and most of the next before I found time to talk to him. I was angry with him and let him know it, but he just sat there beaming at me, his grin a perfect copy of prot's know-it-all smirk. As he was heading back to his room on Ward Two he turned and proclaimed, "Prot says one more task and I'll be cured, too."

"*I'll* decide that, goddamn it!" I shouted after him.

ONE of the night nurses told me later that the Duchess had begun to take some of her meals in the dining room with the other patients. She was shocked and offended by all the belching and farting (courtesy, primarily, of Chuck), but, to her great credit, she usually stuck it out.

At her first appearance Bess tried to get up and serve her. One glance from prot and she returned to her place. As usual, however, she wouldn't eat anything until everyone else had finished.

"How did he get her to come to the table?" I asked the nurse.

"She wants to be the one who gets to go with him," came the obvious reply. She sounded envious.

Session Twelve

WHILE prot was munching peaches and plums I brought up the subject of Howie and his tasks. I explained that the first one he had assigned to him (to find the "bluebird of happiness") had produced a positive effect not only on Howie, but on the rest of the ward as well. Though it had turned out successfully also, the second (to "cure" Ernie) was more problematical. I asked him if he had anything else in mind for my patient.

"Only one final task."

"Do you mind telling me what it is?"

"That would spoil the surprise."

"I think we've had enough surprises around here for a while. Can you guarantee this task will cause no harm to anyone?"

"If he does it well, it will be a very happy day for everyone, including yourself." I was not so certain about that, but my doubts were swallowed up by his self-confidence.

My father once lay down on the living room floor and asked me to make a run at him. He wanted me to push off on his knees, flip over him, and land on my feet above his head. It sounded like suicide. "Trust me," he said. So I put my life in his hands, made a run at him, and, with his help, miraculously landed on my feet. I never did it again. Prot had the same "trust me" look in his eyes when he told me about Howie's last task. And on that note we began our twelfth session.

The minute I started to count, prot fell into a deep trance. I asked whether he could hear me.

"Of course."

"Good. Now I want you to think back to the year 1979; that is, 1979 on Earth. It's Christmas Day, 1979. Where are you and what do you see?"

"I am on the PLANET TERSIPION in what you would call the CONSTELLATION TAURUS. I see orange and green everywhere. I love it. I just love it. The flora on this WORLD are not chlorophyll-based as they are on EARTH and K-PAX. Instead, light is gathered by a pigment similar to that of your red algae. The sky is green because of the chlorine in the atmosphere. There are all kinds of interesting beings, most of whom you would characterize as insects. Some are bigger than your dinosaurs. All of them are quite slow-moving, fortunately, but you have to—"

"Excuse me, prot. I would love to hear about this planet, and all the other places you have visited, but right now I would prefer to concentrate on your passages to Earth."

"Anything you say. But you asked me where I was and what I was doing on christmas of 1979."

"Yes I did, but only as a point of reference. What I'd like to ask you to do now is to come forward in time to your next visit to Earth. Can you do that?"

"Of course. Um, let's see. January? No, I was still on TERSIPION. February? No. I was back on K-PAX then, learning to play the patuse, though I'll never be any good at it. It must have been in march. Yes, it *was* march, that delightful time in your northern hemisphere when the ice on the streams is melting and the mayapples and crocuses are coming up."

"This is March 1980?"

"Precisely."

"And he called you?"

"Well, not for anything in particular. He just wants someone to talk things over with now and then."

"Tell me about him. What's he like? Is he married?"

"Yes, he's married to a girl he knew in—oh, I told you about that already, didn't I?"

"The Catholic girl who was pregnant when they were seniors in high school?"

"What a memory! She's still a catholic, but no longer pregnant. That was five and a half years ago."

"I've forgotten her name."

"I never told you her name."

"Can you tell me now?"

After a lengthy hesitation, during which he seemed to study my haircut (or the need thereof), he said, quietly, "sarah."

Barely concealing my elation: "Did they have a son or a daughter?"

"Yes."

"I mean which?"

"You should do something about that sense of humor, doctor brewer. A daughter."

"So she's about five?"

"Her birthday is next week."

"Any other children?"

"No. Sarah developed endometriosis and they gave her a hysterectomy. Stupid."

"Because she was so young?"

"No. Because there is a simple treatment for it that your medical people should have figured out long ago."

"Can you tell me the daughter's name? Or is that a secret?"

After only a moment's hesitation: "rebecca." When this was divulged so readily I wondered whether Pete had relented and had decided to allow prot to tell me his real name. Perhaps he was beginning to trust me! But prot must have anticipated my question: "Forget it," he said.

"Forget what?"

"He's not going to tell you that."

"Why not? Will he at least tell why not?"

"No."

"Why not?"

"You'll just use the answer to chip away at him."

"All right. Then tell me this: Do they live in the same town he was born in?"

"Yes and no."

"Can you be more specific?"

"They live in a trailer outside of town."

"How far outside of town is it?"

"Not far. It's in a trailer park. But they want to get a house farther out in the country."

A shot in the dark: "Do they have a sprinkler?"

"A what?"

"A lawn sprinkler."

"In a trailer park?"

"All right. Do they both work?"

His mouth puckered slightly, as if the fruit hadn't agreed with him. "He has a full-time job, as you would call it. She earns some money making children's clothing."

"Where does your friend work?"

"The same place his father and his grandfather did. Just about the only place in town there is to work, unless you're a grocer or a banker."

"The slaughterhouse?"

"Yessir, the old butchery."

"What does he do there?"

"He's a knocker."

"What's a 'knocker'?"

"The knocker is the guy who knocks the cows in the head so they don't struggle so much when you cut their throats."

"Does he like his job?"

"Are you kidding?"

"What else does he do? At home, for example?"

"Not much. He reads the newspaper in the evening, after his daughter has gone to bed. On weekends he tinkers with his car and watches tv like everybody else in town."

"Does he still hike in the woods?"

"Sarah would like him to do that, but he doesn't."

"Why not?"

"It depresses him."

"Does he still collect butterflies?"

"He threw out his collection a long time ago. There was no room for it in the trailer."

"Does he regret his decision to get married and raise a family?"

"Oh, no. He is truly devoted to his wife and daughter, whatever that means."

"Tell me about his wife."

"Cheerful. Energetic. Dull. Like most of the housewives you see at the a&p."

"And the daughter?"

"A carbon copy of her mother."

"Do they all get along well?"

"They idolize one another."

"Do they have a lot of friends?"

"None."

"None?"

"Sarah's a catholic. I told you—it's a small town. . . ."

"They never see anyone else?"

"Only her family. And his mother."

"What about his sisters?"

"One lives in alaska. The other is just like everyone else in town."

"Would you say he hates her?"

"He doesn't hate anyone."

"What about male friends?"

"There ain't none."

"What about the bully and the kid he beat up on?"

"One is in prison, the other was killed in lebanon."

"And he never stops off at a tavern after work for a beer with his fellow knockers?"

"Not anymore."

"He did earlier?"

"He used to joke around with the others, have a beer or two. But whenever he invited someone for supper, they always found some excuse not to come. And no one ever invited him and his family for a barbecue or anything else. After a while he began to get the idea. Now they stick to their trailer most of the time. I tried to tell him this would happen."

"Sounds like a pretty lonely existence."

"Not really. Sarah has a million brothers and sisters."

"And now they're going to buy a house?"

"Maybe. Or build one. They've got their eye on a few acres of land. It's a beautiful spot, a part of a farm that someone split up. It has a stream and a couple of acres of trees. A lovely place. Reminds me of home. Except for the stream."

"Tell him I hope he gets it."

"I'll do that, but he still won't tell you his name."

At that point Mrs. Trexler barged in, out of breath, whispering frantically about a disturbance in the psychopathic ward: Someone had kidnapped Giselle! I quickly hushed her up and reluctantly brought prot back from his hypnotic state, left him with Mrs. T, and took off for the fourth floor.

Giselle! It is hard to express the feelings I had in the few seconds it took me to make it downstairs. I couldn't have been more distressed if it had been Abby or Jenny in the hands of whichever lunatic had grabbed her. I saw her slouched down in my office chair, heard her childish voice, smelled her sweet, piney scent. Giselle! All my fault. All my fault. Allowing a helpless girl to "cruise the corridors" of the psych ward. I tried not to imagine a pair of hairy arms wrapped around her neck, or worse. . . .

I banged into Four. Everyone was milling around or chatting amiably, some even beginning to return to their regular routines. I couldn't believe how unconcerned they seemed to be. All I could think of was: What kind of people are these?

The kidnapper's name was Ed. He was a handsome, white, fifty-year-old man who had gone berserk six years earlier and gunned down eight people with a semiautomatic rifle in a shopping mall parking lot. Until that time he had been a successful stockbroker, a model husband and father, sports

161

fan, church elder, six-handicap golfer, and all the rest. Afterward, even with regular medication, he suffered periods of episodic dyscontrol accompanied by significant electrical activity in his brain, which usually ended with utter exhaustion and fists bloodied by pounding them against the walls of his room.

But it wasn't Giselle he had kidnapped. It was La Belle.

I never did find out whether Mrs. Trexler's tongue had slipped or whether I misheard her—I had been worried about Giselle's safety all along. In any case the kitten had gotten into the psychopathic ward, and when the orderlies opened Ed's door to take away his dirty laundry, she slipped inside. It wasn't long before he was banging on the bars of his window and threatening to wring La Belle's little neck unless he could talk to "the guy from outer space."

Villers was there to remind me that he had opposed the idea of having animals in the wards, and perhaps he was right—this would never have happened without the kitten and, furthermore, if anything happened to it, the effect on Bess and the others could be quite demoralizing. I thought Ed was bluffing; he was not in one of his violent phases. But I could see no compelling reason not to let him talk briefly with prot, and I asked Betty to send for him. Prot, however, was already there. Apparently he had followed me down the stairs.

There was no need to explain the situation, only to tell him to assure Ed there would be no reprisal if he let the kitten go. Prot, requesting that no one accompany him, headed for Ed's room. I assumed they would talk through the barred v indow, but suddenly the door opened and prot darted inside, slamming it behind him.

After a few minutes I cautiously approached the window and peered into the room. They were standing over by the far

162

wall, talking quietly. I couldn't hear what they were saying. Ed was holding La Belle, stroking her gently. When he glanced toward me I backed off.

Prot finally came out, but without the kitten. After making sure the security guard had locked Ed's door, I turned to him, puzzled. Anticipating my question, he said, "He won't harm her."

"How do you know that?"

"He told me."

"Uh huh. What else did he tell you?"

"He wants to go to K-PAX."

"What did you tell him?"

"I said I couldn't take him with me."

"What did he say to that?"

"He was disappointed until I told him I would come back for him later."

"And that satisfied him?"

"He said he would wait if he could keep the kitten."

"But—"

"Don't worry. He won't hurt her. And he won't cause you any more trouble, either."

"How can you be so sure of that?"

"Because he thinks that if he does, I won't come back for him. I would anyway, but he doesn't know that."

"You would? Why?"

"Because I told him I would. By the way," he said as we were walking out together, "you'll need to find a few more furry beings for the other wards."

HERE was Howie's final task: to be ready for anything. To respond at a moment's notice to whatever prot, without warning, might challenge him with.

For a day or two he raced at tachyon speed from the

library to his room and back to the library—same old Howie. He didn't sleep for forty-eight hours. He was reading Cervantes, Schopenhauer, the Bible. But suddenly, as he was darting past the lounge window where he had spotted the bluebird, he stopped and took his old seat on the ledge. He began to chuckle, then to roar. Pretty soon the whole ward, except perhaps for Bess, was giggling, then the whole hospital, staff and all. The absurdity of prot's charge, that he be ready for anything that might possibly happen, had sunk in.

"It is stupid to try to prepare for life," Howie told me later, on the lawn. "It happens, and there isn't a damn thing you can do about it." Prot was over by the side wall examining a sunflower. I wondered what he saw in it that we didn't.

"What about your task?" I asked him.

"Qué será, será," he whistled, leaning back to soak up the warm sunshine. "I think I'll take a nap."

I suggested he think about the possibility of moving to Ward One. "I'll wait until Ernie's ready," he said.

The problem was that Ernie didn't want to leave. I had already proposed, at the last staff meeting, that Ernie be transferred to One as well. He had shown no sign of the debilitating phobia since his "cure"—no mask, no complaints about the food, no hog-tying himself at night or sleeping on the floor. He was, in fact, spending most of his time with the other patients, particularly Bess and Maria. He had already become quite adept at recognizing the latter's various alters, learning all their names and characteristics, waiting patiently for the "real" Maria to make an appearance, then going out of his way to keep her around, gently encouraging her interests in needlepoint and macramé. It was obvious that Ernie had a talent for helping others, and I encouraged him to consider going into one of the health or social professions. His reply was, "But there's so much that needs to be done *here.*"

It was about this time that Chuck organized an essay contest to decide who would be the one to go with prot on August seventeenth. The plan called for submission of all entries by August tenth, a week before his "departure," a date that was rapidly approaching. Prot had apparently agreed to read all the essays by the seventeenth.

Several staff members noted that Ward Two was unusually quiet during that two-week period with everyone sitting off by him/herself, thinking hard, bending over periodically to write something down. The only patients who didn't seem to want to go to K-PAX were Ernie and Bess—Ernie because there was work to be done here, and Bess because she felt she didn't deserve a free trip. And, of course, Russell, who called the contest "the work of the devil."

Session Thirteen

E VER since she ran off to Texas with a guitar player at the age of fifteen, my daughter Abby has been a vegetarian. She won't wear fur, either, and has long opposed the use of animals in medical research. I have tried many times to explain to her the benefits to mankind of the latter endeavor, but her mind is closed on the subject. "Explain that to all the dead dogs," is her standard reply. We haven't discussed the subject in years.

Abby once gave me a tape recording of whale songs. At the beginning of session thirteen, while prot was digging into a watermelon, I played it for him. He stopped chewing and tilted his head to one side, much as Shasta had done when she had heard the same tape. By the time it was over he was grinning even more broadly than usual. A piece of the rind was stuck in his teeth. I said, "Can you make anything out of that?"

"Of course."

"What is it? Is it some kind of communication?"

"What did you think it was—stomach gas?"

"Can you tell me what they're saying?"

"Sure."

"Well?"

"They're passing on all kinds of very complex navigational data, temperature and solute and food type and distribution charts, and lots of other things, including some poetry and art. It is rich in imagery and emotion, which you would probably dismiss as 'sentimental.' "

"Can you give me a literal translation of all that?"

"I could, but I won't."

"Why not?"

"Because you would use it against them."

I felt a certain amount of resentment at being held personally responsible for the decimation of many of the world's cetaceans, but could think of no good reply.

"There was also a message for all the other beings on the PLANET." He paused here, peering at me out of the corner of an eye, and took another bite of fruit.

"Well? Are you going to tell me what it was? Or are you going to keep that a secret, too?"

"They're saying, 'Let's be friends.' " He finished the melon, counted, "One-two-three-four-five," and was out like a light.

"Comfortable?" I said, when I realized he had already hypnotized himself.

"Perfectly, my dear sir."

"Good." I took a very deep breath. "Now I'm going to give you a specific date, and I want you to remember where you were and what you were doing on that day. Do you understand?"

"Jawohl."

"Excellent." I braced myself. "The date is August seventeenth, 1985."

There was no hint of shock or other emotion. "Yes," was all he said.

"Where are you?"

"I'm on K-PAX. Harvesting some kropins for a meal."

"Kropins?"

"Kropins are fungi. Something like your truffles. Big truffles. Delicious. Do you like truffles?"

I was a bit annoyed by his attention to trivia at a time like this, though it was I who had pursued the topic. "I've never had truffles. But let's get on with this, shall we? Is anything else happening? Any calls from Earth?"

"There it is now, as a matter of fact, and I'm on my way."

"What did it feel like when the call came?"

"He needed me. I felt that he needed me."

"And how long will it take you to get to Earth?"

"No time at all. You see, at tachyon speed, time goes backward, so that—"

"Thank you. You've already explained to me all about light travel."

"Funny, I don't remember doing that. But then you must know it takes no time at all."

"Yes. I had forgotten. So now you are on Earth?"

"Yes. In zaire."

"Zaire?"

"It is pointing toward K-PAX at this moment."

"And now you'll be heading for—"

"And now I am with him."

"Your friend?"

"Yes."

"Where are you? What is happening?"

"By a river in back of his house. It is dark. He is taking off his clothes."

"He called you to Earth to go for a nighttime swim with him?"

"No. He is trying to kill himself."

"Kill himself? Why?"

"Because something terrible has happened."

"What happened?"

"He doesn't want to talk about it."

"Damn it, I'm trying to help him."

"He knows that."

"Then why won't he tell me?"

"He feels terribly hurt and ashamed. He doesn't want you to know."

"But I can't help him unless he tells me what happened."

"He knows that, too."

"Then why—"

"Because then you'd know what even *he* doesn't want to know."

"Do *you* know what happened?"

"No."

"No? Doesn't he tell you everything that happens to him?"

"Not anymore."

"Then will you help him? If you can get him to tell me what happened you would be taking the first step toward helping him deal with it."

"No."

"Why not?"

"He doesn't want to talk about it—remember?"

"But time's running out for him!"

"Time is running out for everyone."

"All right. What is happening now?"

"He is floating down the river. He is drowning. He wants to die." Prot stated this matter-of-factly, as if he were a disinterested observer.

"Can't you stop him?"

"What can I do?"

"You could talk to him. Help him."

"If he wants to die, that's his right, don't you think?"

"But he is your friend. If he dies you will never see him again."

"I *am* his friend. That is why I won't interfere."

"All right. Is he still conscious?"

"Barely."

"But still in the water?"

"Yes."

"There is still time. Help him, for God's sake."

"There is no need. The stream has washed him onto the bank. He will survive."

"How far downstream did it carry him?"

"Just a few jarts—a mile or so."

"What is he doing now?"

"He's coughing. He's full of water, but he's coming around."

"And you are with him?"

"As close as I am to you right now."

"Can you talk to him?"

"I can talk to him, but he won't talk to me."

"What is he doing now?"

"He's just lying there." At this point prot took off his shirt and lay it on the floor in front of him.

"You covered him?"

"He is shivering." Prot lay down on the carpet beside his shirt.

"You are lying down beside him?"

"Yes. We are going to sleep now."

"Yes, you do that. And now I'm going to ask you to come forward in time to the next morning. The sun is up. Where are you now?"

"Still lying here."

"He is sleeping?"

"No. He just doesn't want to get up."

"Did he say anything during the night?"

"No."

"Did you say anything to him?"

"No."

"All right. Now it's late afternoon. Where are you now?"

Prot got up and returned to his chair. "In zaire."

"Zaire? How did you get to Zaire?"

"It's difficult to explain. You see, light has certain—"

"What I meant was, why did you go back there? Is your friend with you?"

"It looked like a beautiful country. I thought some sightseeing might cheer him up."

"Did you talk to him about it?"

"Yes. I said, 'Let's get out of here.'"

"What did he say?"

"Nothing."

"So now you're in Zaire."

"Yes."

"Both of you."

"Yes."

"What will you do next?"

"Get to know the beings here."

"And then what?"

"We'll move on to another place."

"All right. It's six months later. February seventeenth, 1986. Where are you?"

"Egypt."

"Still in Africa?"

"It's a big continent. By EARTH standards, anyway."

"Is your friend still with you?"

"Of course."

"What did you use for money on these travels?"

"Nothing. We just took what we needed."

"And nobody objected?"

"Not after I explained who we were."

"All right. It's one year after you left the river. August seventeenth, 1986. Where are you now?"

"Sweden."

"Do you like it there?"

"Very much. They are more like K-PAXians here than anywhere else we've been."

"In what way?"

"They are less warlike, and more tolerant toward their fellow beings than the other countries we have visited."

"August seventeenth, 1987."

"Saudi arabia."

"August seventeenth, 1988."

"Queensland, australia."

"August seventeenth, 1989."

"Bolivia."

"October seventeenth, same year."

"The united states. Indiana."

"December seventeenth."

"New york."

"February seventeenth, 1990."

"The long island psychiatric hospital."

"May seventeenth."

"The manhattan psychiatric institute."

"The present."

"Same old place."

"And your friend hasn't spoken to you in all this time?"

"Not a word."

"Have you tried to talk to *him*?"

"Occasionally."

"May I try?"

"Be my guest."

"I need a name. It would be so much easier if you would give me a name to call him."

"I can't do that. But I'll give you a hint. He can fly."

"Fly? Is his name Fred?"

"C'mon, you can do better than that. Can't you think of anything that flies besides airplanes?"

"He's a bird? He has the name of a bird?"

"Bingo!"

"Uh, uh, Donald? Woody? Jonathan Livingston?"

"Those aren't real birds, are they, gene?"

"Martin? Jay!"

"You're getting waaaaaarmerrrrrr!"

"Robin? Robert?"

"Well done, doctor brewer. The rest is up to you."

"Thank you. I'd like to speak to him now. Do you mind?"

"Why should I?" Suddenly prot/Robert slouched down in his chair. His hands fell limply to his sides.

"Robert?"

No response.

"Robert, this is Doctor Brewer. I think I can help you."

No response.

"Robert, listen to me. You've had a terrible shock. I understand your pain and suffering. Can you hear me?"

No response.

At this point I took a chance. Knowing prot and, through him, something about Robert, I could not shake the feeling that if he had in fact hurt, or killed, someone, it must have been an accident or, more likely perhaps, self-defense. It was mostly speculation, but it was all I had. "Robert, listen to me. What happened to you could have happened to anyone. It is not something to be ashamed of. It is a normal response that human beings are programmed to carry out. It's in our genes. Do you understand? Anyone might have done the same thing you did. Anyone would condone what you did and why you did it. I want you to understand that. If you will just acknowledge that you hear me we can talk about it. We don't have to talk about what happened just yet. Only about how we can get you to overcome your grief and self-hatred. Won't you talk to me? Won't you let me help you?"

We sat silently for several minutes while I waited for Robert to make a move, a small gesture to indicate he had heard my plea. But he never twitched a muscle.

"I'm going to ask you to think about it for a while. We'll talk about this again a week from today, all right? Please trust me."

No response.

"I'm going to ask to speak with your friend now."

In a twinkling prot was back, wide-eyed and smiling broadly. "Hiya, gene. Long time no see. How ya been?" We talked a bit about our first few meetings back in May, the tiniest details of which he described perfectly, as if he had a tape recorder inside his head.

I woke him and sent him back to Ward Two. Cheerful as ever, he didn't remember a thing about what had just transpired.

★ ★ ★

THERE was a seminar that afternoon in our lecture room, but I didn't hear a word of it. I was considering the possibility of increasing the number of sessions with prot/Robert. Unfortunately, I had a meeting in Los Angeles at the end of that week and the beginning of the next, something that had been arranged months before and would have been impossible to get out of. But I suspected that even a dozen more sessions wouldn't be enough. Maybe a hundred wouldn't be enough to sort everything out. True, I now knew his first name, but I wasn't sure this would be of much help in tracing his background. It was encouraging in another sense, however: It indicated a possible crack in the armor, a hint of willingness on Robert's part to begin to cooperate, to help with his own recovery, to get well. But there were only two weeks left before prot's "departure." If I couldn't get through to him by then, I was afraid it would be too late.

"HIS name is Robert Something," I told Giselle after the seminar.

"Great! Let me check it against my list." She bent over a long computer printout. Her profile was perfect, like one of those "Can you draw me?" advertisements. "Here's one! But this guy disappeared in April of 1985, and he was sixty-eight years old. Wait! Here's another one! And he disappeared in August! No, no, he was only seven then. That would make him twelve now." She looked at me sadly. "Those were the only two Roberts."

"I was afraid of that."

"He's *got* to exist," she wailed. "There has to be a record of his existence. We must have missed something. An important clue . . ." She jumped up and began pacing around my office. Eventually she spotted the picture of my family on my desk. She asked me about my wife, where we had met, and so on. I told her how long I had known Karen, a little about the kids. Then she sat down and told me some things about herself she hadn't mentioned before. I shall not record the details here, but she was on intimate terms with more than one prominent figure from the worlds of sports and journalism. The point, however, is that although she had countless male friends, she had never married. I wasn't about to ask her why, but she answered as if I had: "I'm an idealist and a perfectionist and all the wrong things," and turned her gaze to a faraway place in the distant past. "And because I have never met a man I could give myself to, utterly and completely." Then she turned to me. In a moment of helpless ego—Brown's syndrome is a very powerful force—I was sure she was going to say, "Until now." My tie suddenly needed my attention. "And now I'm going to lose him," she whimpered, "and there's nothing I can do about it!" She was in love with prot!

Caught between disappointment and relief I said something stupid: "I've got a son you might like." I was thinking of Fred, who had just landed a part in a comedy playing at a dinner theater in Newark. She smiled warmly.

"The pilot who decided to become an actor? How old was he when that picture was taken?"

"Nineteen."

"He's cute, isn't he?"

"I suppose so." I gazed fondly at the photograph on my desk.

"That picture reminds me of my own family," she said. "My dad was so proud of us. We all became professionals of one sort or another. Ronnie is a surgeon, Audrey's a dentist, Gary a vet. I'm the only dud in the bunch."

"I wouldn't say that. Not at all. You are one of the best reporters in the country. Why settle for second best in something else?"

176

She smiled at that and nodded. "And that picture of you reminds me of my father."

"How so?"

"I don't know. He was nice. Kind. You'd have liked him."

"I probably would have. May I ask what happened to him?"

"He committed suicide."

"Oh, Giselle, I'm very sorry."

"Thank you." Dreamily: "He had cancer. He didn't want to be a burden."

We sat in my office thinking our own private thoughts until I happened to glance at the clock on my desk. "Good grief—I've got to run. We're going to go see Freddy perform tonight. He's playing a reporter. You want to come with us?"

"No, no thanks. I've got some writing to do. And some thinking."

As we got into the elevator I reminded her that I was going out of town for a few days and wouldn't be back until the middle of the following week.

"Maybe I'll have the case solved by then! I'm supposed to get the locations of all the slaughterhouses tomorrow!"

She got off on Two and I stood there in the empty elevator feeling the tug of gravity and a profound sense of sadness and not knowing which I understood less.

Session Fourteen

I didn't get back to my office until the following Wednesday morning. As soon as I walked in I detected the fragrance of pine trees, and I knew that Giselle had been there. Perched on top of the great mound of work piled on my desk was a note neatly handwritten in green ink:

> *There was only one disappearance in 1985 that occurred in a town where a slaughterhouse is located. It was in South Carolina, and the missing person was a woman. Am spending this week in the library going over newspaper files for that year.*
>
> *See you later.*
>
> *Love,*
> *G.*

While I was reading it I got a call from Charlie Flynn, the astronomer, my son-in-law's colleague at Princeton.

After he had returned from his vacation in Canada, Steve had told him about the discrepancy between his and prot's account of the orbit of K-PAX around its double suns. He was very excited. The calculation, he said, had been done by one of his graduate students. Upon hearing of prot's version he had recalculated the orbital pattern himself, and it turned out to be exactly as prot had described it: a pendulum-like back-and-forth motion, not a figure eight. All the star charts prot had drawn up were quite accurate as well. I thought nothing would faze me anymore where prot was concerned, but what this trained scientist said next shocked me as much as it fascinated him. He said, "Savants are basically people with prodigious memories, aren't they? This is different. There is no way anyone could guess that orbital pattern or intuit it. I know this sounds crazy, but I can't see how he could have come up with this information unless he had actually been there!" This from a man who is as sane as you or I. "Could I talk to your patient?" he went on. "There are several thousand questions I'd like to ask him!"

I rejected this idea, of course, for a number of reasons. I suggested, however, that he send me a list of fifty of the key questions he wanted to ask prot, and assured him that I would be happy to present them to him. "But make it fast," I said. "He claims he's leaving on August seventeenth."

"Can you get him to stay longer?"

"I doubt it."

"Can you try?"

"I'm trying my damnedest," I assured him.

THE rest of the morning was taken up with meetings and an interview with the third candidate for the directorship. I'm afraid I didn't give him the attention he deserved. He seemed capable enough, and had published some excellent work. His specialty was Tourette's syndrome, and he suffered from a mild form of the affliction himself—nervous tics, primarily, though he occasionally called me "a piece of shit." But I was too preoccupied with trying to formulate a way to get through to Robert to listen. At last an idea came to mind, and unforgivably I sat up and blurted, "Ah!" Thinking I was referring to his discourse, our guest was quite pleased by my outburst and went on and on with an even greater display of facial twitching and name calling than before. I paid no attention to him—I was absorbed by the question: *Could the host personality be hypnotized while the secondary alter is already under hypnosis?*

"OKAY, ready for anything," prot said after finishing a huge mixed fruit salad and blowing his nose on his napkin. He tossed it into the bowl and looked for the spot on the wall behind me. Knowing he would jump the gun, however, I had covered it up before he could throw himself into a trance.

"I'm not going to hypnotize you for a while."

"I told you it wouldn't work," he said, breaking into the all-too-familiar grin.

"I want to talk to you about Robert first."

The smile vanished. "How did you find out his name?"

"You told me."

"Under hypnosis?"

"Yes."

"Well, flatten my feet and call me daffy."

"What happened to his wife and child?"

Prot seemed confused, edgy. "I don't know."

"Oh, come on. He must have told you *that*."

"Wrong. He's never mentioned them since I found him by the river."

"Where are they now?"

"I have no idea."

Either prot was lying, which I strongly doubted, or he was genuinely unaware of Robert's activities when he wasn't around. If that were the case the latter could try almost anything—possibly even suicide—without prot's knowledge. I was more certain than ever that I had to get through to Robert as soon as possible. In fact, there wasn't a moment to lose. I stood up and removed the tape from the spot on the wall behind me. Prot fell into his usual deep trance immediately.

"We are now in the present. Prot? Do you understand?"

"Yes. It is not a difficult concept."

"Good. Is Robert there with you?"

"Yes."

"May I speak to him, please?"

"You may, but he probably won't speak to *you*."

"Please let him come forward."

Silence. Robert slouched down in the chair, his chin on his chest.

"Robert?"

No response.

"Robert, this is Doctor Brewer. Please open your eyes."

There was a barely detectable shift in his position.

"Robert, listen to me. I am not just *trying* to help you. I *know* I can help you. Please trust me. Open your eyes!"

His eyes flickered open for a moment, then closed again. After a few seconds he blinked several times, as if vacillating, and finally they stayed open. It was little more than a vacant stare, but it was something.

"Robert! Can you hear me?" After what seemed like an eternity I detected a hint of a nod. "Good. Now I want you to focus your attention on the spot on the wall behind me."

The lifeless eyes, gazing emptily at the edge of my desk, shifted upward slightly.

"A little higher. Raise your eyes a little higher!"

Slowly his focus lifted, an inch at a time, slowly, slowly. Ignoring my presence completely, he lifted his gaze to the wall behind my shoulder. His mouth had fallen open.

"Good. Now, listen carefully. I'm going to count forward from six to ten. As I count, your eyelids will become heavy and you will grow increasingly sleepy. By the time I get to ten, you will be in a deep trance. But you will be able to hear and understand everything I say. Now this is very important: When I clap my hands, you will wake up. Do you understand?"

A tiny, but definite, nod.

"Good. We'll begin now. Six . . ." I watched carefully as his eyelids began to droop. ". . . and ten. Robert, can you hear me?"

No response.

"Robert?"

Unintelligible.

"Please speak louder."

A feeble "Yes," more like a gurgle. But someone was there! At that moment I was very, very glad I had chosen to become a psychiatrist.

"Good. Now listen to me. We are going to travel back in time. Imagine the pages of a calendar turning rapidly backward. It is now August eighth, 1989, exactly one year ago. Now it is 1988; now 1987, now 1986. Now, Robert, it is August eighth, 1985, at noon. Where are you?"

He remained motionless for several minutes before murmuring, "I am at work." He sounded tired, but his voice was clear, though slightly higher-pitched than prot's.

"What are you doing there?"

"I am eating my lunch."

"What are you eating?"

182

"I have a Dutch loaf sandwich with Miracle Whip and pickles, a peanut butter sandwich with Concord grape jelly, potato chips, a banana, two sugar cookies, and a thermos of coffee."

"Where did you get your lunch?"

"From my lunch bucket."

"Your wife made it for you?"

"Yes."

"All right. We are going to move forward eight days and two hours. It is 2:00 P.M. on August sixteenth, 1985. Where are you now?"

"At work."

"And what are you doing at this moment?"

"Knocking steers."

"All right. What do you see?"

"It is jerking around making noises. I bang it again. Now it is still." He wiped some imaginary perspiration from his forehead with the back of his hand.

"And it moves down the line where someone else cuts the throat, is that right?"

"Yes, after it is shackled."

"Then what?"

"Then another one comes along. Then another, then another, then another—"

"All right. Now it is just after quitting time. You are on your way home from work. You are home now, getting out of your car. You are going up the walk—"

His eyes widened. "Someone is there!"

"Who? Who is there?"

Agitated: "I don't know. He is coming out of my house. I have never seen him before. He is going back into the house! Something is wrong! I am running after him, chasing him into the house. Oh, God, No! NOOOO-

OOOOOOOOOO!" He began to wail, his head wagging back and forth, his eyes as big as the moon. Then he looked toward me and his demeanor changed radically—an utter transmogrification. He looked as though he wanted to kill me.

"Robert!" I yelled, clapping my hands together as loudly as I could. "Wake up! Wake up!" His eyes closed immediately, thank God, and an exhausted Robert sat slumped in the chair in front of me.

"Robert?"

No response.

"Robert?"

Still nothing.

"Robert, it's all right. It's over now. Everything is all right. Can you hear me?"

No response.

"Robert, I'd like to talk to prot now."

No response.

"Please let me speak to prot. Prot? Are you there?" I was beginning to feel a mounting trepidation. Had I been too aggressive? What if—?

Finally his head lifted and his eyes blinked open. "Now you've done it."

"Prot? Is that you?"

"You had to do it, didn't you? Just when he started to trust you, you went for the jugular."

"Prot, I would like to have taken it more slowly, but you are planning to leave us on the seventeenth. Our time is almost up!"

"I told you—I have no choice in the matter. If we don't leave then we'll never be able to get back."

"You and Robert?"

"Yes. Except . . ."

"Except what?"

"Except he's gone now."

"Gone? Gone where?"

"I don't know."

"Look hard, prot. He must be there with you somewhere."

"Not anymore. He's not here anymore. You have driven him away."

"Okay, I'm going to count back from five to one now. As the numbers decrease you will begin to wake up. On the count of one you will be fully alert and feeling fine. Ready? Five . . . one."

"Hello."

"How do you feel?"

"I think I had too much fruit. Have you got any antacid?"

"Betty will get some for you later. Right now we need to talk."

"What else have we been doing for the past three months?"

"Where is your friend Robert right now?"

"No idea, coach."

"But you told me earlier he was in 'a safe place.' "

"He was then, but he's gone now."

"But you could contact him if you wanted to."

"Maybe. Maybe not."

"All right. Let's review a few things. When you came to Earth five years ago, Robert was trying to drown himself. Remember?"

"How could I forget?"

"But you don't know why?"

"I think it's because he didn't want to live anymore."

"I mean, you have no idea what caused him to be so upset? So desperate?"

"Haven't we been over this?"

"I think he may have killed someone."

"Robert? Nah. He loses his temper sometimes, but—"

"I don't think he meant to kill anyone. I think he caught someone in his house. Someone who may have harmed his wife and daughter in some way. He is only human, prot. He reacted without thinking."

"I'm not surprised."

"Prot, listen to me. You helped Howie to cure Ernie of his phobia. I'm going to ask you to do something for me. I'm going to ask you to cure Robert. Let's call it a 'task.' I'm assigning you the task of curing Robert. Do you accept the assignment?"

"Sorry, I can't."

"Why the hell not?"

"Ernie wanted to get well. Robert doesn't. He just wants to be left alone. He doesn't even want to talk to *me* anymore."

"You've helped a lot of the patients in Ward Two. I have confidence that if you really put your mind to it you could help Robert, too. Will you please try?"

"Anything you sigh, mite. But don't hold your breath."

"Good. I think that's enough work for today. We both need a little time to reflect on this. But I'd like to schedule an extra session with you on Sunday. It's the only day I have. Would you be willing to come back for a Sunday session?"

"What about your promise to your wife?"

"What promise?"

"That you would take sundays off, no matter what. Except that you cheat and bring work home."

"How did you know about that?"

"Everyone knows about that."

"She's going to the Adirondacks with Chip for a couple of weeks, if it's any of your business."

"In that case, I would be delighted to accept your kind invitation."

"Thank you."

"Don't mention it. Is that all?"

"For now."

"Toodle-oo."

I switched off the tape recorder and slumped down in my chair, as drained of emotion as Robert must have been. I felt very bad about this particular session. I had rushed things, taken a big chance and failed, perhaps irreversibly. One thing you learn in psychiatry: Treating a psychotic patient is like singing opera—it seems easy enough to the spectator, but it takes a tremendous amount of work and there are no short-cuts.

On the other hand, perhaps I had not been bold *enough*. Perhaps I should have forced him to tell me exactly what he saw that August afternoon when he got home from work. I knew now that he had stumbled onto something terrible, and I suspected what it might have been. But this hadn't helped my patient one iota and, indeed, may have made things worse. Moreover, I had missed a golden opportunity to ask him his last name! The position of director, free of patient responsibility, suddenly seemed a very attractive idea.

JUST before she left for the weekend Betty told me she had given up on the idea of motherhood. I said I was sorry it hadn't worked out for her. She replied that I needn't be, and pointed out that there were already more than five billion human beings on Earth, and maybe that was enough. She had obviously been talking with prot.

As we were walking down the corridor she suggested that I stop in and see Maria. She wouldn't tell me why. I glanced at my watch. I had about five minutes before I had to leave for a fund-raising dinner at the Plaza. Sensing my impatience, she patted my arm. "It'll be worth it."

I found Maria in the quiet room talking with Ernie and Russell. She seemed uncharacteristically happy, so I thought it was a new alter I had encountered. But it was Maria herself! Although the answer was obvious, I asked her how she was feeling.

"Oh, Doctor Brewer, I have never felt so good. All the others are with me on this. I know it."

"With you on what? What happened?"

"I've decided to become a nun! Isn't it wonderful?" I found myself smiling broadly. The idea was so simple I wondered why I hadn't thought of it myself. Perhaps because it was *too* simple. Perhaps we psychiatrists have a tendency to make things more complicated than they really are. In any case, there she was, nearly beside herself with joy.

I was beginning to feel better myself. "What made you decide to do that?"

"Ernie showed me how important it was to forgive my father and my brothers for what they did. After that, everything was different."

I congratulated Ernie on his help. "It wasn't my idea," he said. "It was prot's."

Russell seemed unsure about what to make of all this. "It is only by Beelzebub, the prince of demons, that this man casteth out demons," he mumbled uncertainly, and shuffled away.

188

Maria watched him leave. "Of course it's only for a little while."

"Why only for a while?" I asked her.

"When prot comes back he's going to take me with him!"

Session Fifteen

KAREN and Shasta left for the Adirondacks late Sunday morning. Shaz was as joyous as Maria had been two days earlier—she knew exactly where she was going. I promised to join them in a week or so.

Chip, busy with his lifeguard duties, had decided not to spend his time with his fuddy-duddy parents after all, but moved in with a friend whose father and mother were also on vacation. With no one in the house but me, I decided to check into the guest room at the hospital for the duration.

I made it to my office that afternoon just in time for my session with prot. I was already sweating profusely. It was a very hot day and the air conditioning system wasn't working. It didn't seem to bother prot, who had stripped down to his polka-dot boxer shorts. "Just like home," he chirped. I turned on the little electric fan I keep for such emergencies, and we got on with it.

Unfortunately, I cannot relate the contents of that interview verbatim because of a malfunction in my tape recorder, which I did not discover until the session was over. What follows is a summary based on the sweaty notes I took at the time.

While he devoured a prodigious number of cherries and nectarines, I handed him the list of questions Charlie Flynn had faxed to me for prot's attention. I had perused the fifty undoubtedly well-chosen queries myself, but they were quite technical and I wasn't much interested at that point what his responses, if any, would be. (I could have answered the one about light travel—it's done with mirrors.) Prot merely smiled and stuffed them under the elastic band of his shorts alongside the ever-present notebook.

At the merest suggestion he found the spot on the wall behind me and immediately fell into his usual deep trance. I wasted no time in dismissing prot and asked to speak with Robert. His countenance dropped at once, he slouched down to the point where it almost seemed he would fall out of his chair, and that's where he stayed for the remainder of the hour. Nothing I brought up—his father's death, his relationship with his friends (the bully and his victim), his employment at the slaughterhouse, the whereabouts of his wife and daughter—elicited the slightest hint of a reaction. I carefully introduced the subject of the lawn sprinkler, but even that evoked no response whatsoever. It was as if Robert had prepared himself for this confrontation, and nothing I could say was going to shock him out of his virtually catatonic state. I tried every professional maneuver and amateurish trick I could think of, including lying to him about what prot had told me about his life, and ending up by calling him a shameless coward. All to no avail.

But something had occurred to me when I brought up the subject of his family and friends. I recalled prot, and was greatly relieved when he finally showed up. I asked him whether there was anyone, if not me, Robert would be willing to speak to. After a minute or two he said, "He might be willing to talk to his mother."

I implored him to help me find her. To give me a name or an address. He said, again after a few moments of silence, "Her name is beatrice. That's all I can tell you."

Before I woke him up I tried one more blind shot. "What is the connection between a lawn sprinkler and what happened to Robert on August seventeenth, 1985?" But he seemed genuinely befuddled by this reference (as had the un-hypnotized prot), and there was no sign of the panic elicited by my wife's turning on ours at the Fourth of July picnic in our back yard. Utterly frustrated, I brought him back to reality, called in our trusty orderlies, and reluctantly sent him back to Ward Two.

THE next day Giselle reported that she had spent most of the previous week, along with her friend, at the Research Library tracking down and reading articles from small-town (those with slaughterhouses) newspapers for the summer of 1985, so far without success, though there were still two large trays of microfilm to go. I passed on the meager information I had managed to obtain. She doubted that Robert's mother's name would be of much help, but it led her to another idea. "What if we also search the files for 1963, when his father died? If there's an obituary for a man whose wife's name was Beatrice and who had a six-year-old son named Robert . . . Damn! Why didn't I think of that before?"

"At this point," I agreed, "anything's worth a try."

CHUCK had collected all the "Why I Want to Go to K-PAX" essays over the weekend. Most of the patients had submitted one, and a fair number of the support staff as well, including Jensen and Kowalski. As it happened, this was the time for Bess's semiannual interview. During that encounter I asked her why she hadn't entered the contest.

"You know why, Doctor," she replied.

"I would rather you tell me."

"They wouldn't want somebody like me."

"Why not?"

"I don't deserve to go."

"What makes you think that?"

"I eat too much."

"Now, Bess, everyone here eats more than you do."

"I don't deserve to eat."

"Everyone has to eat."

"I don't like to eat when there are so many that don't have anything. Every time I try to eat I see a lot of hungry faces pressed up against the window, just watching me eat, waiting for something to fall on the floor, and when it does they can't get in to pick it up. All they can do is wait for somebody to take out the garbage. I can't eat when I see all those hungry faces."

"There's nobody at the window, Bess."

"Oh, they're there all right. You just don't see them."

"You can't help them if you're starving, too."

"I don't deserve to eat."

We had been around this circle many times before. Bess's battle with reality had not responded well to treatment. Her periods of depression had been barely managed with ECT and Clozaril and, more recently, by the presence of La Belle Chatte. She perked up a little when I told her that Betty was planning to bring in another half dozen cats from the animal shelter. Until further progress was made in the treatment of paranoid schizophrenia and psychotic depression there wasn't much more we could do for her. I almost wished she had been among those who had submitted an application for passage to K-PAX.

The kitten, incidentally, was doing fine with Ed. The only problem was that everyone in the psychopathic ward now wanted an animal. One patient demanded we get him a horse!

O N Tuesday, August fourteenth, prot called everyone to the lounge. It was generally assumed he was going to make some kind of farewell speech and announce the results of the essay contest Chuck had organized. When all of Wards One and Two and some of Three and Four, including Whacky and Ed and La Belle, had gathered around, along with most of the professional and support staff, prot disappeared for a minute and came back with—a violin! He handed it to Howie and said, "Play something."

Howie froze. "I can't remember how," he said. "I've forgotten everything."

"It will come back," prot assured him.

Howie looked at the violin for a long time. Finally he placed it under his chin, ran the bow across the strings, reached for the rosin that prot had thoughtfully provided, and immediately broke into a Fritz Kreisler étude. He stopped a few times, but *didn't* start over and try to get it perfect. Grinning like a monkey he went right into a Mozart sonata. He played it pretty badly, but, after the last note had faded into perfect silence, the room broke into thunderous applause. It had been the greatest performance of his career.

With one or two exceptions the patients were in a fine mood all that day. I suppose everyone was on his best behavior so as not to jeopardize his chances for an all-expense-paid trip to paradise. But prot made no speech, no decision on a space companion. Apparently he was still hoping to talk Robert into going with him.

Oddly, no one seemed particularly disappointed. Everyone knew it was only a matter of days—hours—until "departure" time, and his selection would have to be made by then.

Session Sixteen

DESPITE facing what should have been a very long and presumably exhausting journey prot seemed his usual relaxed self. He marched right into my examining room, looked around for his basket of fruit. I switched on my backup tape recorder and checked to see that it was working properly. "We'll have the fruit at the end of today's session, if you don't object."

"Oh. Very well. And the top o' the afternoon to ye."

"Sit down, sit down."

"Thankee kindly, sir."

"How's your report coming?"

"I'll have it finished by the time I leave."

"May I see it before you go?"

"When it's finished. But I doubt you'd be interested."

"Believe me, I would like to see it as soon as possible. And the questions for Dr. Flynn?"

"There are only so many hours in a day, gino, even for a K-PAXian."

"Are you still planning to return to your home planet on the seventeenth?"

"I must."

"That's only thirty-eight hours from now."

"You're very quick today, doctor."

"And Robert is going with you?"

"I don't know."

"Why not?"

"He's still not talking to me."

"And if he decides not to accompany you?"

"Then there would be room for someone else. You want to go?"

"I think I'd like that some day. Right now I've got a lot of things to do here."

"I thought you'd say that."

"Tell me—how did you know that Robert might want to go back with you when you arrived on Earth five years ago?"

"Just a hunch. I had a feeling he wished to depart this world."

"What would happen exactly if neither of you went back on that date?"

"Nothing. Except that if we didn't go back then, we never could."

"Would that be so terrible?"

"Would you want to stay here if you could go home to K-PAX?"

"Couldn't you just send a message that you're going to be delayed for a while?"

"It doesn't work that way. Owing to the nature of light . . . Well, it's a long story."

"There are plenty of reasons for you to stay."

"You're wasting your time," he said, yawning. I had been told that he hadn't slept for the last three days, preferring instead to work on his report.

The moment had come for my last desperate shot. I wondered whether Freud had ever tried this. "In that case, I wonder if you'd care to join me in a drink?"

"If that's your custom," he said with an enigmatic smile.

"Something fruity, I suppose?"

"Are you insinuating that I'm a fruit?"

"Not at all."

"Just kidding, doc. I'll have whatever you're having."

"Stay right there. Don't move." I retreated to my inner office, where Mrs. Trexler was waiting sardonically with a laboratory cart stocked with ice and liquor—Scotch, gin, vodka, rye—plus the usual accompaniments.

"I'll be right here if you need anything," she growled.

I thanked her and wheeled the cart into my examining room. "I think I'll have a little Scotch," I said, trying to appear calm. "I like a martini before dinner, but on special occasions like this one I prefer something else. Not that there are that many special occasions," I added quickly, as if I were applying for the directorship of the hospital. "And what about you?"

"Scotch is fine."

I poured two stiff ones on the rocks, and handed one to prot. "Bon voyage," I said, raising my glass. "To a safe trip home."

"Thank you," he said, lifting his own. "I'm looking forward to it." I had no idea how long it had been since his last drink, or if he had ever taken one at all, but he appeared to enjoy the first sip.

"To tell you the truth," I confessed, "K-PAX does sound like a beautiful place."

"I think you would like it there."

"You know, I've only been out of this *country* two or three times."

"You should see more of your own WORLD, too. It's an interesting PLANET." He took a deep slug, bared his teeth and swallowed, but his timing wasn't right and he choked and coughed for several seconds. While watching him try to get his breath I remembered the day my father taught me to drink wine. I hated the stuff, but I knew it signified the beginning of adulthood, so I held my nose and gulped it down. My timing wasn't right either, and I spewed some burgundy all over the living room carpet, which retains a ghostly stain to this day. I'm not sure he ever forgave me for that. . . .

"You don't hate your father," prot said.

"What?"

"You've always blamed your father for the inadequacies you perceive in yourself. In order to do that you had to hate him. But you never really hated him. You loved your father."

"I don't know who told you all of this, but you don't know what you're talking about."

He shrugged and was silent. After a few more swallows (he wasn't choking anymore) he persisted: "That's how you rationalized ignoring your children so you could have more time for your work. You told yourself you didn't want to make the same mistake as your father."

"I didn't ignore my children!"

"Then why do you not know that your son is a cocaine addict?"

"What? Which son?"

"The younger one. 'Chip,' you call him."

There *had* been certain signs—a distinct personality change, a constant shortage of funds—signs I chose to disregard until I found time to deal with them. Like most parents I didn't want to know that my son was a drug addict, and I was just putting off finding out the truth. But I certainly didn't want to learn about the problem from one of my patients. "Anything else you want to get off your chest?"

"Yes. Give your wife a break and stop singing in the shower."

"Why?"

"Because you can't carry a tune in a basket."

"I'll think about it. What else?"

"Russell has a malignancy in his colon."

"What? How do you know that?"

"I can smell it on his breath."

"Anything else?"

"That's all. For now."

We had a few more drinks in total silence, if you don't count the thoughts roaring through my head. This was interrupted, finally, by a tap on the door. I yelled, "Come in!" It was Giselle, back from the library.

Prot nodded to her and smiled warmly. She took his hand and kissed him on the cheek before slipping over and whispering in my ear, "It's Robert Porter. That's about all we know so far." Then she plopped down in the corner chair. I brought her a drink, which she gratefully accepted.

We chatted about inconsequential things for a while. Prot was having a fine time. After his fourth Scotch, when he was giggling at everything anyone said, I shouted, "Robert Porter! Can you hear me? We know who you are!"

Prot seemed taken aback, but he finally realized what I

was doing. "I tol' you an' tol' you," he snorted unhappily. "He ain' comin' out!"

"Ask him again!"

"I've tried. I've rilly rilly rilly tried. What else c'n I do?"

"You can stay!" Giselle cried.

He turned slowly to face her. "I can't," he said sadly. "It's now or never."

"Why?"

"As I a'ready 'splained to doctor bew—bew—doctor brewer, I am shed—shed—I am 'xpected. The window is op'n. I c'n *only* go back on august seventeenth. At 3:31 inna norming."

I let her go on. She couldn't do any worse than I had. "It's not so bad here, is it?" she pleaded.

Prot said nothing for a moment. I recognized the look on his face, that combination of amazement and disgust which meant he was trying to find words she could comprehend. Finally he said, "Yes, it is."

Giselle bowed her head.

I poured him another drink. It was time to play my last trump. "Prot, I want you to stay too."

"Why?"

"Because we need you here."

"Wha' for?"

"You think the Earth is a pretty bad place. You can help us make it better."

"How, f'r cryin' out loud?"

"Well, for example, there are a lot of people right here at the hospital you have helped tremendously. And there are many more beings you can help if you will stay. We on Earth have a lot of problems. All of us need you."

"You c'n help y'rself if you want to. You just hafta *want* to, thass all there is to it."

"Robert needs you. Your friend needs you."

"He doesn't need me. He doesn't even pay 'tention to me anymore."

"That's because he's an independent being with a mind of his own. But he would want you to stay, I know he would."

"How d'you know that?"

"Ask him!"

Prot looked puzzled. And tired. He closed his eyes. His glass tipped, allowing some of his drink to spill onto the carpet. After a long minute or two his eyes opened again. He appeared to be completely sober.

"What did he say?"

"He told me I've wasted enough time here. He wants me to go away and leave him alone."

"What will happen to him when you go? Have you thought about that?"

The Cheshire-cat grin: "That's up to you."

Giselle said, "Please, prot. *I* want you to stay, too." There were tears in her eyes.

"I can always come back."

"When?"

"Not long. About five of your years. It will seem like no time at all."

"Five *years*?" I blurted out in surprise. "Why so long? I thought you'd be back much sooner than that."

Prot gave me a look of profound sadness. "Owing to the nature of time . . ." he began, then: "There is a tradeoff for round trips. I would try to explain it to you, but I'm just too damn tired."

"Take me with you," Giselle pleaded.

He gave her a look of indescribable compassion. "I'm sorry. But next time . . ." She got up and hugged him.

"Prot," I said, emptying the bottle into his and Giselle's glasses. "What if I tell you there's no such place as K-PAX?"

"*Now* who's crazy?" he replied.

AFTER Jensen and Kowalski had taken prot back to his room, where he slept for a record five hours, Giselle told me what she had learned about Robert Porter. It wasn't much, but it explained why we hadn't been able to track him down earlier. After hundreds of hours of searching through old newspaper files, she and her friend at the library had found the obituary for Robert's father, Gerald Porter. From that she learned the name of their hometown, Guelph, Montana. Then she remembered something she had found much earlier about a murder/suicide that had taken place there in August of 1985, and she called the sheriff's office for the county in western Montana where the incident occurred. It turned out that the body of the suicide victim had never been found, but, owing to a clerical error, it had gone into the record as a drowning, rather than a missing person.

The man Robert killed had murdered his wife and daughter. Robert's mother had left town a few weeks after the tragedy to live with his sister in Alaska. The police didn't have the address. Giselle wanted to fly out to Montana to try to find out where she had gone, as well as to obtain pictures of the wife and daughter, records and documents, etc., in case I could use them to get through to Robert. I quickly approved a travel advance and guaranteed payment of all her expenses.

"I'd like to see him before I go," she said.

"He's probably sleeping."

"I just want to watch him for a few minutes."

I understood perfectly. I love to watch Karen sleep, too, her mouth open, her throat making little clicking noises.

"Don't let him leave until I find her," she pleaded as she went out.

I don't remember much about the rest of the afternoon and evening, although reports have it that I fell asleep during a committee meeting. I do know that I tossed and turned all night thinking about prot and about Chip and about my father. I felt trapped somewhere in the middle of time, waiting helplessly to repeat the mistakes of the past over and over again.

GISELLE called me from Guelph the next morning. One of Robert's sisters, she reported, was indeed living in Alaska, the other in Hawaii. Sarah's family didn't have either address, but she (Giselle) was working with a friend at Northwest Airlines to try to determine Robert's mother's destination when she left Montana. In addition, she had gathered photographs and other artifacts from his school years and those of his wife-to-be, thanks to Sarah's mother and the high school principal, who had spent most of the previous night going through the files with her. "Find his mother," I told her. "If you can, get her back here. But fax all the pictures and the other stuff now."

"They should already be on your desk."

I cancelled my interview with the Search Committee. Villers was not pleased—I was the last candidate for the directorship.

There were photos of Robert as a first-grader on up to his graduation picture, with the yearbook caption, "All great men are dead and I'm not feeling well," along with pictures of the wrestling teams and informal snapshots of soda fountains and pizza parlors. There were copies of his birth certificate, his immunization records, his grade transcripts (A's and B's), his citation for top marks in the county Latin contest, his diploma. There were also pictures of his sisters, who had graduated a few years before he had, and some information on them. And one of Sarah, a vivacious-looking blonde, leading a cheer at a basketball game. Finally, there was a photograph of the family standing in front of their new house in the country, all smiles. Judging by the age of the daughter, it must have been taken not long before the tragedy occurred. Mrs. Trexler brought me some coffee as I was gazing at it, and I showed it to her. "His wife and daughter," I said. "Somebody killed them." Without warning she burst into tears and ran from the room. I remember thinking that she must be more sympathetic toward the plights of the patients than I had thought. It wasn't until much later, while paging through her personnel file at the time of her retirement, that I learned her own daughter had been raped and murdered nearly forty years earlier.

I had lunch in Ward Two and laid down the law: no cats on the table. I sat across from Mrs. Archer, who was now taking all her meals in the dining room. She was flanked by prot and Chuck. Both were talking animatedly with her. She looked uncertainly from one to the other, then slowly lifted a spoonful of soup to her mouth. Suddenly, with a sound that could have been heard clear up in Ward Four, she slurped it in. Then she grabbed a handful of crackers and crumbled them vigorously into her bowl. She finished her meal with half the soup smeared all over her leathery face. "God," she said happily, "I've always wanted to do that."

"Next time," said Chuck, "belch!"

I thought I saw Bess smile a little, though it might have been wishful thinking on my part.

After the meal I returned to my office and asked Mrs. Trexler, who had regained her composure, to cancel all my appointments for the rest of the day. She mumbled something unintelligible about doctors, but agreed to do so. Then I went to find prot.

He was in the lounge, surrounded by all the patients and staff from Wards One and Two. Even Russell, who had experienced some sort of revelation after he understood that it was prot who had been responsible for Maria's deciding to become a nun, was there. When I came into the room he exclaimed, "The Teacher saith, My time is at hand." The corners of his mouth were caked with dried spittle.

"Not just yet, Russ," I said. "I need to talk to him first. Will everyone excuse us, please?" I calmed a chorus of protest by assuring them he would be back shortly.

On the way to his room I remarked, "Every one of them would do anything you asked them to. Why do you suppose that is?"

"Because I speak to them as equals. That's something you doctors seem to have a hard time with. I listen to them being to being."

"I listen to them!"

"You listen to them in a different way. You are not as concerned with them or their problems as you are with the papers and books you get out of it. Not to mention your salary, which is far too high."

He was wrong about that, but this wasn't the time to argue the matter. "You have a point," I said, "but my professional manner is necessary in order to help them."

"Let's see—if you believe that, then it must be true. Right?"

"That's exactly what I wanted to talk to you about."

We came to his room, the first time I had been there since his earlier disappearance. It was virtually bare except for his notebooks lying on the desk. "I've got some pictures and documents to show you," I said, spreading the file out on its surface, gently shoving aside his report. A few of the photographs I held back.

He looked over the pictures of himself, the birth and graduation certificates. "Where did you get these?"

"Giselle sent them to me. She found them in Guelph, Montana. Do you recognize the boy?"

"Yes. It is robert."

"No. It is you."

"Haven't we been over this before?"

"Yes, but at that time I didn't have anything to prove that you and Robert were the same person."

"And we aren't."

"How do you explain the fact that he looks so much like you?"

"Why is a soap bubble round?"

"No, I mean why does he look *exactly* like you?"

"He doesn't. He is thinner and fairer than I am. My eyes are light-sensitive and his aren't. We are different in a thousand ways, as you are different from your friend bill siegel."

"No. Robert is you. You are Robert. You are each part of the same being."

"You are wrong. I'm not even human. We are just close friends. Without me he'd be dead by now."

"And so would you. Whatever happens to him also happens to you. Do you understand what I am saying?"

"It is an interesting hypothesis." He wrote something in one of the notebooks.

"Look. Do you remember telling me that the universe

207

was going to expand and contract over and over again, forever?"

"Naturally."

"And you said later that if we were in the contraction phase time would run backward but we'd never know the difference because all we would have would be our memories of the past and a lack of knowledge of the future. Remember?"

"Of course."

"All right. It's the same here. From your perspective Robert is a separate individual. From my perspective the truth is perfectly logical and obvious. You and Robert are one and the same person."

"You misunderstand the reversal of time. Whether it is moving forward or backward, the *perception* is the same."

"So?"

"So it makes no difference whether you are correct or not."

"But you admit the possibility that I'm right?"

His smile widened markedly. "I'll admit that, if you'll admit it's possible that I came from K-PAX."

From his point of view there wasn't the slightest doubt about his background. Given several more months or years I might have been able to convince him otherwise. But there was no more time. I pulled the pictures of Sarah and Rebecca from my pocket. "Do you recognize them?"

He seemed shocked, but only for a moment. "It is his wife and daughter."

"And this one?"

"This is his mother and father."

"Giselle is trying to locate your mother and sister in Alaska. She is going to try to bring your mother here. Please, prot, don't leave until you talk to her."

He threw up his hands. "How many times must I tell you—I have to leave at 3:31 in the morning. *Nothing* can change that!"

"We are going to get her here as soon as we can."

Without looking at a clock he said, "Well, you have exactly twelve hours and eight minutes to do it in."

THAT evening Howie and Ernie threw prot a bon voyage party in the recreation room. There were many gifts for their "alien" friend, souvenirs of his visit to Earth: records, flowers, all kinds of fruits and vegetables. Mrs. Archer hammered out popular tunes on the piano accompanied by Howie on the violin. Cats were everywhere.

Chuck gave him a copy of *Gulliver's Travels*, which he had lifted from the bookshelves in the quiet room. I recalled prot's telling me that the (Earth) story he liked best was "The Emperor's New Clothes." His favorite movies, incidentally, were *The Day the Earth Stood Still*, *2001*, *ET*, *Starman*, and, of course, *Bambi*.

There was a great deal of hugging and kissing, but I detected a certain amount of tension as well. Everyone seemed nervous, excited. Finally, Chuck demanded to know which of them was going to get to go with him. With those crossed eyes I wasn't sure whether he was looking at me or prot. But prot answered, "It will be the one who goes to sleep first."

They all lined up immediately for a last tearful embrace, then dashed to their beds, leaving him alone to finish his report and prepare for his, and hopefully their, journey, each trying desperately to fall asleep with visions of yorts dancing in their heads.

I told him I had some things to do, but would come to say good-bye before he left. Then I retired to my office.

At about eleven o'clock Giselle called. She had found

Robert's sister's address in Alaska. Unfortunately, the woman had died the previous September, and his mother had gone on to live with the other sister in Hawaii. Giselle had tried to reach her, but without success. "It's too late to get her to New York in time," she said, "but if we find her, she might be able to call him."

"Make it fast," I told her.

For the next three hours I tried to work to the accompaniment of *Manon Lescaut* on my cassette player. In Act Three of that opera Manon and Des Grieux depart for the New World, and I understood at last why I love opera so much: Everything that human beings are capable of, all of life's joy and tragedy, all its emotion and experience, can be found there.

My father must have felt this, too. I can still see him lying on the living room sofa on a Saturday afternoon with his eyes closed, listening to the Metropolitan Opera broadcasts. Oh, how I wish he had lived and we had had a chance to talk about music and his grandchildren and all the other things that make life fun and interesting and good! I tried to envision a parallel universe in which he had not died and I had become an opera star, and I imagined singing some of his favorite arias for him while Mother brought out a big Sunday dinner for us to eat.

I suppose I must have dozed off. I dreamed I was in an unfamiliar place where the cloudless purple sky was full of moons and sailing birds, and the land a panoply of trees and tiny green flowers. At my feet stood a pair of huge beetles with humanoid eyes; a small brown snake—or was it a large worm?—slithered along behind them. In the distance I could see fields of red and yellow grains, could make out several small elephants and other roaming animals. A few chimpanzee-like creatures chased one another into and out of a nearby forest. I found myself crying, it was so lovely. But the most beautiful feature of all was the utter silence. There wasn't a hint of wind and it was so quiet I could hear the soft ringing of faraway bells. They seemed for all the world to be tolling, "gene, gene, gene. . . ."

I woke with a start. The clock was chiming 3:00. I hurried down to prot's room, where I found him at his desk writing furiously in his notebook, trying, presumably, to complete his report about Earth and its inhabitants before departing for K-PAX, letting it go until the last minute, it appeared, just as a human being might do. Beside him were his fruits, a stalk or two of broccoli, a jar of peanut butter, the essays and other souvenirs, all neatly packed in a small cardboard box. On the desk, next to his notebooks, were a pocket flashlight, a hand mirror, and the list of questions from Dr. Flynn. All six of the lower-ward cats were lying asleep on the bed.

I asked him whether he minded my looking over the answers he had formulated to those fifty queries. Without interrupting his writing he shook his head and waved me into the other chair.

Some of the questions, e.g., the one about nuclear energy, he had left unanswered, for reasons he had made clear in several of our sessions together. The last item was a request for a list of all the planets prot had visited around the universe, to which he had replied, "See Appendix," which tallied the complete list of sixty-four. This inventory included a brief description of those bodies and their inhabitants, as well as a series of star charts. It was not everything Professor Flynn and his colleagues, including Steve, had hoped for, but enough to keep them busy for some time, no doubt.

At around 3:10 he threw down his pencil, yawned, and stretched noisily as if he had just finished a routine piece of work.

"May I see it?"

"Why not? But if you want to *read* it you'd better make a copy right away—it's the only one I've got." I called one of the night nurses to take it upstairs, admonishing him to get some help and to use all the copiers that were operational. He hurried off, clutching the little notebooks as though they were so many eggs. The possibility of stalling the process occurred to me at that point, but it might well have made matters even worse and I quickly rejected the idea.

I had a feeling the report would be a rather uncomplimentary account of prot's "visit" to Earth, and I asked him, "Is there anything about our planet that you liked? Besides our fruits, I mean."

"Sure," he said, with an all-too-familiar grin. "Everything but the people. With one or two exceptions, of course."

There didn't seem to be much left to say. I thanked my amazing friend for the many interesting discussions and for his success with some of the other patients. In return, he thanked me for "all the wonderful produce," and presented me with the gossamer thread.

I pretended to take it. "I'm sorry to see you go," I said, shaking his brawny hand, though I wanted to hug him. "I owe you a lot, too."

"Thank you. I will miss this place. It has great potential." At the time I thought he was referring to the hospital, but of course he meant the Earth.

The nurse came running back with the copy a few minutes before it was time for prot to leave. I returned the original notebooks, a little jumbled but intact, to prot.

"Just in the nick of time," he said. "But now you'll have to leave the room. Any being within a few feet will be swept along with me. Better take them with you, too," he said, indicating the cats.

I decided to humor him. Well, why not? There wasn't a damn thing I could do about it anyway. I rousted the cats from his bed. One by one they brushed against his leg and streaked for various other warm places. "Good-bye, Sojourner Porter," I said. "Don't get knocked over by any aps."

"Not good-bye. Just *auf wiedersehen*. I'll be back before you know it." He pointed toward the sky. "After all, K-PAX isn't so far away, really."

I stepped out of the room, but left the door open. I had already notified the infirmary staff to stand by, to be prepared for anything. I could see Dr. Chakraborty down the corridor with an emergency cart containing a respirator and all the rest. There were only a couple of minutes to go.

The last I saw of prot he was sitting at his desk tapping his report into a neater stack, checking his flashlight. He placed his box of fruit and other souvenirs on his lap, picked up the little mirror and gazed into it. Then he transferred the flashlight to his shoulder. At that moment one of the security guards came puffing up to tell me that I had an urgent long-distance call. It was Robert's mother! At exactly the same instant, Chuck came running down the hall with his worn little suitcase, demanding to be "taken aboard." Even with all this commotion I couldn't have taken my eyes off prot for more than a couple of seconds. But when I turned to tell him about the phone call, he was already gone!

We all raced into the room. The only trace of him left behind were his dark glasses lying on a scribbled message. "I won't be needing these for a while," the note said. "Please keep them for me."

Acting on my earlier hunch that prot had hidden out in the storage tunnel during the few days he had allegedly gone to Canada, Greenland, and Iceland, we rushed to that area. The door was locked, and the security guard had some difficulty finding the right key. We waited patiently—I was confident we would find prot there—until he finally got the heavy door open and found the light switch. There was enough dusty old equipment to start our own museum, but there was no sign of prot. Nor was he hiding in the surgical theater or the seminar room, or anywhere else we thought he might have tried to conceal himself. It didn't occur to any of us to check the rooms of the other patients.

ONE of the nurses found him a few hours later, lying unconscious and in the fetal position on the floor of Bess's room. He was little more than alive. His eyes were barely dilatable, his muscles like steel rods. I recognized the symptoms immediately—there were two other patients exactly like him in Ward 3B: he was in a deep catatonic state. Prot was gone; Robert had stayed behind. I had rather expected something like this. What I failed to foresee, however, was that later the same morning Bess would also be reported missing.

GISELLE had the report translated by a cryptographer she knew, who used as a basis for this the pax-o version of *Hamlet* that prot had done for me earlier. Titled "Preliminary observations on B-TIK (RX 4987165.233)," it was primarily a detailed natural history of the Earth, especially of the recent changes thereon, which he attributed to man's "cancerous" population growth, his "mindless" consumption of its natural resources, and his "catastrophic" elevation of himself to superiority over all the other species who cohabit our planet. All of this is consistent with his use of capitals for the Earth and other planets, and lower case for individual beings.

There were also some suggestions as to how we might "treat" our social "illnesses": the elimination of religion, capital, nationalism, the family as the basic social and educational unit—all the things he imagined were fundamentally wrong with us and, paradoxically, the things most of us hold dear. Without these "adjustments," he wrote, the "prognosis" was not good. Indeed, he gave us only another decade to make the "necessary" changes. Otherwise, he concluded, "human life on the PLANET EARTH will not survive another century." His last four words were somewhat more encouraging, however. They were: *Oho minny blup kelsur*—"They are yet children."

Epilogue

R OBERT'S mother arrived with Giselle the day after
prot's departure and stayed through the weekend, but there
was no indication whatever of cognizance on Robert's part.
She was a lovely woman, a bit confused, of course, about
what had happened to her son—from the beginning she had
been completely unaware of prot's existence—as were we all.
I told her there was no need for her to stay longer, and promised to let her know of any change in his condition. I dropped
her at Newark Airport before heading for the Adirondacks
with Chip, who tearfully admitted his cocaine problem when
I confronted him with it, to join Karen and Bill and his wife
and daughter.

T H A T was nearly five years ago. How I wish I could tell you
that Robert sat up one fine day during that time and said,
"I'm hungry—got any fruit?" But, despite our best efforts and
constant attention, he remains to this day in a deep catatonic

state. Like most catatonics he probably hears every word we say, but refuses, or is unable, to respond. Perhaps with patience and kindness on our part he will recover, in time, from this tragic condition. Stranger things have happened. I have known patients who have returned to us after twenty years of "sleep." In the meantime, we can do little more than wait.

Giselle visits him almost every week, and we usually have lunch and talk about our lives. She is currently researching a book about the deplorable infant mortality rate in America. Her article on mental illness featuring prot and some of the other patients appeared in a special health-oriented issue of *Conundrum*. As a result of that piece we have received thousands of letters from people asking for more information about K-PAX, many of them wanting to know how they can get there. And a Hollywood producer has requested authorization to do the story of Robert's life. I don't know whether anything will come of that, but, thanks to Giselle's tireless efforts, the information we received from Robert's mother, the hours of conversations I had with prot, and the cooperation of the authorities in Montana, we now have a reasonably clear picture of what happened on that terrible afternoon of August sixteenth through the early morning hours of August seventeenth, 1985. First, some biographical details.

Robert Porter was born in Guelph, Montana, 1957, the son of a slaughterhouse worker. Shortly after Robert's birth his father became disabled when a convulsing steer became unshackled and fell on top of him. In terrible pain for the rest of his life, unable even to tolerate bright light, he spent many of his waking hours with his young son, an energetic, happy boy who liked books and puzzles and animals. He never recovered from his injuries and succumbed when Robert was six years old.

His father had often speculated about the possibility of

217

remarkable life forms living among the stars in the sky and Robert called into being a new friend from a faraway planet where people didn't die so readily. For the next several years Robert suffered brief bouts of depression, at which times he usually called on "prot" for comfort and support, but he was never hospitalized or otherwise treated for it.

His mother took a job in the school cafeteria, which paid poorly, and the family, which also included two daughters, was barely able to make ends meet. Luxuries, like fresh fruit, were rare. Recreation took the form of hikes in the nearby woods and along the riverbank, and from these Robert gained a love and appreciation of the flora and fauna in forest and field and, indeed, of the forests and fields themselves.

He was a good student, always willing to pitch in and help others. In the fall of 1974, when he was a high school senior, Robert was presented a community service medal by the Guelph Rotary Club and, later that year, was elected captain of the varsity wrestling team. In the spring of 1975 he was awarded a scholarship to the state university to study field biology. But his girlfriend, Sarah Barnstable, became pregnant and Robert felt obligated to marry her and find work to support his new family. Ironically, the only job he could find was the one that had killed his father some twelve years earlier.

To add to their difficulties his wife was Catholic, and the resulting mixed marriage stigmatized the pair in the eyes of the residents of their small town, and they had few, if any, friends. This may have been a factor in their eventual decision to move to an isolated valley some miles outside of town.

One August afternoon in 1985, while Robert was stunning steers at the slaughterhouse, an intruder appeared at the Porter home. Mother and daughter were in the backyard cooling themselves under the lawn sprinkler. The man, a stranger who had been arrested and released numerous times for a variety of crimes, including burglary, automobile theft, and child molestation, entered the house through the unlocked front door and watched Sarah and little Rebecca from the kitchen window until the girl came inside, probably to use the bathroom. It was then that the intruder accosted her. Hearing her daughter's screams the mother ran into the house, where both she and Rebecca were raped and murdered, though not before Sarah had severely scratched the intruder's face and nearly bitten off one of his ears.

Robert arrived home just as the man was coming out of the house. On seeing the husband and father of his victims the murderer ran back inside and out the rear door. Robert, undoubtedly realizing that something was terribly wrong, pursued him into the house, past the bloody bodies of his wife and daughter lying on the kitchen floor, and into the yard, where he caught up with their killer and, with the strength of a knocker and the skills of a trained wrestler, broke the man's neck. The sprinkler was still on, and remained so until the police shut it off the next day.

He then returned to the house, carried his wife and daughter to their bedrooms, covered them with blankets, washed and dried their swimsuits and put them away, mopped the bloody floor, and, after saying his final farewells, made his way to the nearby river, where he took off his clothes and jumped in, an apparent suicide attempt. Although his body was never found, the police concluded that he had died by drowning, the case was officially closed, and that is how the report went into the files.

He must have come ashore somewhere downstream, and from that point on he was no longer Robert, but "prot" (derived, presumably, from "Porter"), who wandered around the country for four and a half years before being picked up at the bus terminal in New York City. How he lived during that period is a complete mystery, but I suspect he spent a lot of time in public libraries studying the geography and languages of the countries of the world, in lieu of actually visiting them. He probably slept there as well, though how he found food and clothing is anybody's guess.

But who was prot? And where did his bizarre idea of a world without government, without money, sex, or love come from? I submit that somehow this secondary personality was able to utilize areas or functions of the brain that the rest of us, except, perhaps, those afflicted with savant syndrome and certain other disorders, cannot. Given that ability, he must have spent much of his time developing his concept of an idyllic world where all the events that had accumulated to ruin his "friend" Robert's life on Earth could not happen. His vision of this utopian existence was so intense and so complete that, over the years, he imagined it down to the most minute detail, and in a language of his own creation. He even divined, somehow, the nature of its parent suns and the pattern of stars in the immediate vicinity, as well as those of several other planets he claimed to have visited (all the data he provided to Dr. Flynn and his associates have proven to be completely accurate).

His ideal world had to be one in which fathers don't die while their children are growing up. Prot solved this problem in two ways: A K-PAXian child rarely, if ever, sees his parents, or even knows who they are; at the same time, he is comforted by the knowledge that they will probably live to be a thousand.

It had to be a world without sex, or even love, those very human needs which can destroy promising young lives and rewarding careers. More importantly: Without love there can be no loss; without sex, no sex crimes. A world without even water, which might be used for sprinkling lawns!

There would be no currency of any kind in this idealized place, the need for which kept Robert out of college and forced him to spend his life destroying the creatures he loved, the same kind of work that had killed his father. As a corollary, no animals would be slaughtered or otherwise exploited on his idyllic planet.

His world would be one without God or any form of religion. Such beliefs had prevented Sarah from using birth-control devices, and then had stigmatized the "mixed marriage" in the eyes of the community. Without religion such difficulties could never arise. He may also have reasoned that what happened to Robert's wife and child, and his father as well, argued against the existence of God.

Finally, it had to be a world without schools, without countries, without governments or laws, all of which prot saw as doing little, if anything, to solve Robert's personal and social problems. None of the beings on his idealized planet were driven by the forces of ignorance and greed that, in his eyes, motivate human beings here on Earth.

I was puzzled at first by the question: Given his intolerable situation, why didn't Robert move with his pregnant wife to another part of the state or country, both for work and to escape the local bigotry? It was Giselle, a small-town girl herself, who reminded me that young people all over America, trapped by family ties and economic need, accept jobs they abhor and stay put for the rest of their lives, benumbing themselves on their off hours with beer and sports and soap operas.

But, despite this dreary prospect, it is possible that without the terrible events of August sixteenth through seventeenth, 1985, Robert and his wife and daughter might have enjoyed a reasonably happy life together. They certainly maintained strong family ties, both with one another and with their respective kin. But something did happen that day, something so devastating as to deal the final blow to Robert's psyche. He called on his alter ego one last time to help him deal with that unspeakable horror.

But this time prot was unable to heal the wounds, at least not anywhere on Earth, where rape and murder are of no more consequence than last night's television shows. In prot's mind the only place where one could deny such horrible crimes was the imaginary world he had created, where violence and death are not a way of life. A beautiful planet called K-PAX, where life is virtually free of pain and sorrow.

He spent the next five years trying to convince Robert to go there with him. Instead, devastated by grief and guilt, he retreated farther and farther into his own inner world, where even prot could not follow.

Why prot chose to "return" after exactly that period of time is unclear, particularly in view of the fact that his earlier visits were of much shorter duration. He may have realized that it would take considerable time to convince Robert to accompany him on his return, discovering finally that even the allotted five years wouldn't be enough. In any case prot did, indeed, depart this Earth (for all practical purposes) at the appointed time, and Robert is still with us in Ward 3B.

The staff and patients bring him fruit every day, and recently I brought in a Dalmatian puppy, who never leaves his side except to go outside, all of which he ignores. Hoping to stimulate his curiosity I tell him about all the new patients who have arrived over the past few years, including a brand-new Jesus Christ, whom Russell welcomed to Ward Two with, "I was you, once." Upon arrival all of them are told "the legend of K-PAX," which, along with the gossamer thread, brings smiles and hope and makes our job a little easier.

I also keep Robert up to date on the activities of Ernie and Howie, both of whom have been released and are leading highly productive lives, Ernie as a city-employed counselor for the homeless and Howie as a violinist with a New York–based chamber ensemble. The former, who until recently had never even kissed a woman for fear of contamination, is now engaged to be married. Both stop by MPI frequently to say hello to me and to Robert and the other patients, and Howie has performed for all of us on a number of occasions.

I've told him also about the wedding of Chuck and Mrs. Archer, who are happily sharing a room in Ward Two, not because they have to remain on that floor but because they choose to wait there for prot's return. Mrs. A, who is no longer called "the Duchess," looks much younger now, but I'm not sure whether it's because of the marriage or her giving up smoking. And about their "adopting" Maria, who has moved into a convent in Queens and is the happiest novice out there. She is totally free of headaches and insomnia, and none of her secondary identities has put in an appearance since she left the hospital.

Russell comes to pray with Robert daily. He has recovered completely from the surgical removal of a golf ball-size tumor in his colon, and so far there has been no sign of a recurrence.

Ed is doing well, too. There have been few violent episodes since prot's departure, all minor, and he has been transferred to Ward Two. He spends most of his time working in the flower gardens with La Belle Chatte.

All of them are waiting patiently for prot's return and the journey to K-PAX. Except for Whacky, who was recently reunited with his former fiancée when her husband was returned to prison for a lengthy stay. To my knowledge no one has told Robert about this, but perhaps, as prot undoubtedly would have, he just knows.

Perhaps he knows also that Mrs. Trexler is retired now. On my recommendation she has been seeing a psychoanalyst, and she tells me she is more at peace with herself than she has been in decades.

And that Betty McAllister became pregnant shortly before prot's departure, and is now the mother of triplets. Whether he had anything to do with this I can't say.

Of course I've also told him about my daughter Abby's new job, now that her kids are both in school, as editor of the Princeton-based *Animal Rights Forum*—prot would have liked that. And about Jenny, now a resident in internal medicine at Stanford, who plans to stay in California to work with AIDS patients in the San Francisco area. Her sexual preference and disinclination to produce grandchildren for us seems of microscopic importance compared to her dedication to helping others, and I am *very* proud of her. As I am of Freddy, who is appearing at the time of this writing in a Broadway musical. He lives in Greenwich Village with a beautiful young ballerina, and we've seen more of him in the last year than in all those he was an airline pilot combined.

But I'm proudest of all of Will (he doesn't want to be called "Chip" anymore), who has taken an interest in Bill and Eileen Siegel's daughter and calls her every day, much to the delight of the phone company. I have brought him to the hospital once or twice to show him what his old man does for a living, but when he met Giselle he decided he wanted to become a journalist. We are very close now, much more so than I was with Fred and the girls. For that, as with so many other things, I have prot to thank.

And of course I brag about my two grandsons, whom I get to see quite often—they are Shasta's favorite visitors—and

224

who are the smartest and nicest kids I've ever known, with the possible exception of my own children. I'm proud of all of them.

I gave up the chairmanship to Klaus Villers. Despite his decree limiting the number of cats and dogs in the hospital to six per floor he is doing a far better job than I ever could have done. Now, unencumbered by all administrative duties and the talk show and as much of the other extraneous baggage as possible, I spend my working hours with my patients, and most of my free time with my family. I no longer sing at the hospital Christmas party, but my wife insists I continue to do so in the shower—she says she can't sleep otherwise. We both know I'm no Pavarotti, but I still think I sound a lot like him, and perhaps that's all that matters.

I wish I could tell Robert that Bess is all right, but she has never turned up, nor have the flashlight, mirror, box of souvenirs, etc., and we have no idea as to her whereabouts. If you see a young black woman with a pretty face, perhaps sitting on a park bench hugging herself and rocking, please help her if you can and let us know where she is.

And of course I dearly wish I could tell him where his friend prot has gone. I have played for him all the tapes of our sessions together, but there is no sign of comprehension on his part. I tell him to wait a little longer, that prot has promised to return. He hears all this, curled up on his cot like some chrysalis, without batting an eye. But perhaps he understands.

Will prot ever show up again? And how did he get from his room to Bess's under our very noses? Did this involve a kind of hypnosis on his part, or a similar ability we don't comprehend? We may never know. I fervently wish I could talk with him again, just for a little while, to ask him all the questions I never got the chance to ask before. I still think we could have learned a great deal more from prot and, perhaps, from all our patients. As the cures to many of our physical ailments may be waiting for us in the rain forests, so may the remedies for our social ills lie in the deepest recesses of our minds. Who knows what any of us could do if we were able to concentrate our thoughts with prot's degree of intensity, or if we simply had sufficient willpower? Could we, like him, see ultraviolet light if we wanted to badly enough? Or fly? Or outgrow our "childhood" and create a better world for all the inhabitants of the EARTH?

Perhaps he *will* return some day. By his own calculations he is due again soon. Giselle, who has been waiting patiently for him, has no doubts whatsoever, nor do any of the patients, nor most of the staff, who keep his dark glasses on the little dresser beside Robert's bed. And sometimes at night I go out and look up at the sky, toward the constellation Lyra, and I wonder. . . .

Acknowledgments

I am indebted to many individuals for their generous assistance, especially John Davis, M.D. for helpful discussions, and Rea Wilmshurst, C. A. Silber, Burton H. Brody, and Robert Brewer for critical readings of the manuscript. I also thank my editors Robert Wyatt and Iris Bass for their enormous skill and excellent advice, Ida Giragossian for suggesting I give them a try, Annette Johnson and Susan Abramowitz for their selfless efforts on my behalf, and my agent Maia Gregory for her wit and timely encouragement. And, as always, my wife Karen for her unflagging support of everything I have ever done.

Glossary

Å—angstrom (one ten-millionth of a millimeter)

ABREACTION—release of emotional tension brought about by recalling a repressed traumatic experience

ADRO—a K-PAXian grain

AFFECT—the emotional state or demeanor of a psychiatric patient

AGAPE—a star in the constellation Lyra

AIKIDO—a Japanese form of self-defense involving the throwing of one's opponent

ANAMNESIS—the recollection of past events

AP—a small, elephant-like being

APHASIA—inability to speak or understand spoken or written language

BALNOK—a large-leafed K-PAXian tree

BROT—an orf (a progenitor of the dremers)

c—the speed of light (186,000 miles per second)

CHOREA—a disease of the nervous system characterized by jerky, involuntary movements

CONFABULATION—the replacement of a gap in one's memory by something he or she believes to be true

COPROPHILIA—an obsession with feces

DELUSION—a false belief that is resistant to reason or confrontation with actual fact

DRAK—a red grain having a nutty flavor

DREMER—a K-PAXian of prot's species

ELECTROCONVULSIVE THERAPY (ECT)—electric shock treatment used in cases of acute depression

ELECTROENCEPHALOGRAM (EEG)—a graphical representation of the electrical activity of the brain

EM—a large, frog-like being who lives in trees

FLED—an undescribed K-PAXian being

FLOR—an inhabited planet in the constellation Leo

HOM—a K-PAXian insect

HYPNOSIS—an induced trance-like state producing vivid recollection along with an enhanced susceptibility to outside suggestion

JART—a measurement of distance (equivalent to 0.214 miles)

K-MON—one of the two suns of K-PAX (also called Agape)

KORM—a bird-like being

K-PAX—a planet in the constellation Lyra

KREE—a K-PAXian vegetable, much like a leek

K-RIL—one of the suns of K-PAX (also called Satori)

KROPIN—a truffle-like fungus

LIKA—a K-PAXian vegetable

MANO—a dremer

MOT—a skunk-like animal

MULTIPLE PERSONALITY DISORDER (MPD)—a psychological dysfunction characterized by the existence of two or more distinct personalities, any of which may be in command of the body at a given time

NARR—a doubter

NEUROLEPTIC DRUG—a compound having antipsychotic properties

NOLL—a planet in the constellation Leo

ORF—one of the progenitors of the dremers

PARANOIA—a mental disorder characterized by feelings of persecution

PATUSE—a K-PAXian musical instrument, similar to the bass viol

PROT—traveler

RELDO—a village on the planet K-PAX

RULI—a cow-like being

SATORI—a star in the constellation Lyra

SAVANT SYNDROME—a condition characterized by remarkable mental capabilities, usually associated with a low level of general intelligence

SWON—an em

TERSIPION—a planet in the constellation Taurus

THON—a K-PAXian grain

TOURETTE'S SYNDROME—a neurological disorder characterized by recurrent involuntary movements, and sometimes by grunts, barks, or epithets

TROD—a chimpanzee-like being

YORT—a sugar plum

10340   Dawson / 6-99 —